Bloodline

Joe Jiménez

PIÑATA
BOOKS

PIÑATA BOOKS
ARTE PÚBLICO PRESS
HOUSTON, TEXAS

Bloodline is funded in part by grants from the City of Houston through the Houston Arts Alliance and the Texas Commission on the Arts. We are grateful for their support.

Piñata Books are full of surprises!

Arte Público Press
University of Houston
4902 Gulf Fwy, Bldg 19, Rm 100
Houston, Texas 77204-2004

Cover design by John-Michael Perkins
Cover photo by Eloísa Pérez-Lozano

Library of Congress Cataloging in Publication Control Number:
2015050270 (print)

Printed in the United States of America
April 2016–May 2016
Versa Press, Inc., East Peoria, IL

10 9 8 7 6 5 4 3 2 1

Praise for *Bloodline*

"A haunting, beautiful story about the vulnerability and heartbreak of young adulthood. Jiménez' lyrical novel will resonate with teen and adult readers alike."　　　　　—Reyna Grande, author of *The Distance Between Us*

"A punch in the gut, *Bloodline* is an exceptional debut novel. Joe Jiménez's killer literary instinct, his precision of language, his mastery of story is second to none. There is no young adult novel quite like this one. It challenges the way we think about masculinity, family and love."

—Virginia Grise, author of *blu*

"Joe Jiménez' debut YA novel is beautiful in the hardest way—luminous and poetic, heartbreaking and violent. *Bloodline* is the story of 17-year-old Abram and all the questions he's grappling with—family and relationships, school and the future, loneliness and dreams, and all the struggles that come with trying to discover who he really is and who he wants to be. In the outside world, Abram fights with his fists, and on the inside, he fights to listen to the inner voice urging him towards life."

—ire'ne lara silva, author of *Blood Sugar Canto*

"Pay attention to this novel. It's a story that provocatively asks if we need fathers to be men. Jiménez's storytelling offers up a grandma who wears manpants, Abram who throws fists full of hard questions and a game-changing Uncle Claudio who together play out a surprising answer for readers. With his spectacular visual poeticism, his strong representation of place and an excellent command of voices underrepresented in literature, Jiménez expertly delivers the heart wrenching blow-by-blow of this important tale."

—Richard Villegas, Jr., author of *La Música Romántica*

"This lyrical debut novel documents an entire ocean that is a young man's inner beauty struggling to balance between interminable, raging and violent seas. In gorgeous language portraits that only a poet like Jiménez can unapologetically conjure, where a room stands as still as an arm bone, and where all the world becomes light and silence, this contemporary Hamlet-inspired story features a Claudio, an Ophelia, a Polonius in Afghanistan and living and non-living men who intersect with each other and with the inevitable destiny that is their bloodline. This is a complex and honest portrayal of angst inside the mind of a brilliant and sensitive teenager who is in love, who is bursting with vision and who allows his bones to breathe new life as he tragically remembers his one wild and precious life."

—Natalia Treviño, author of *Lavando la Dirty Laundry*

for Sophia and Santiago

1

"He needs a father," you hear your grandmother tell her friend Becky. At the square table in the center of the little kitchen, the two sit, sipping *manzanilla* tea and picking at pineapple bread. Your grandmother's thumbs are at her temples, rubbing. Her voice is quiet, like a bird sitting on a fence just before morning.

With her man pants on and her teeth holding back rough words, Becky says, "Why?"

"I don't want him to be lost."

In the hall by the green square bathroom, near the light switch that glows orange at night and the painting of Saint Michael, you stand where no one can see you. Seventeen. It is the year you learned how to drive stick, the year you felt love for the very first time, like a gray balloon expanding inside your chest. Seventeen. The year you fought Willie P., Gabriel, George and Jacob—all before Thanksgiving. Four fights, two suspensions. And they said: "He's lost his last chance."

It is 11 p.m., and you are supposed to be asleep. But when you'd put your head to the pillow, anxiety overcame you, thudding and thumping and twirling itself in your brain and your arms, in the hollow box of your chest and in your knees, which quivered on your old mattress. Alone in your room, all you felt like was to get up, to not sleep, to stand in the hall and listen to your grandmother and her girlfriend whispering about you in the kitchen.

It is 11 p.m., and your heart is rapping its knuckles on your throat.

The wall behind you is yellow. It holds up your spine. The floor is a ghost; its echoes swallow your ankles and feet. So you stand very still, like a light post or maybe a pylon in a parking lot, a pylon made of yellow cement, designed to keep things from crashing into other things. You should be sleeping now, your face buried in bed-sheets and dreamland, a pillow holding your thoughts. But sleep is some flame-filled thing you want no part of.

"Another fight," your grandmother mumbles to Becky, who gently pushes aside your grandmother's gray braid to knead the stony knot in her shoulder. The sound of your grandmother's syllables shrinks, and you can hear the sadness fall from her sobs, which are soft, like a handful of cotton balls.

"Not all boys need fathers. Better to have no man around than to have a bad one, don't you think?"

The spoon that holds your grandmother's sugar clinks against her cup.

A father? You scoff, the back of your head pressing against the wall. Underneath the painting of Saint Michael vanquishing a demon, your blood fist-pumps vigorously in your throat and behind your eyes, and your mouth is as dry as a dune.

The kitchen is quiet.

Beneath you, the floor, coldly and knowingly, holds you.

Your feet sweat. You fear they'll stick to the floor.

"The counselor told me this was his last chance. What can I do? I don't want him lost. Or to drop out."

With a hardness that is almost inescapable, almost impossible to contain, the fear leaks out. It is hard for you to stomach the miry slur of your grandmother's tears. Knowing you've caused them jabs at your throat.

"He needs a man. I can't do this, Becky. We can't. I can't. Not on my own."

∾ ∾ ∾

A year ago, your grandmother hung the Saint Michael over the dark hole in the wall you punched one afternoon when everything seemed small and lightless and unfair and wicked. By Saint Michael, in the hall, with the pale yellow wall behind your heart, no one can see you, barefoot, one hand swollen and pressed against your chest like you held something there, some coin or toy or a small shield. Against the stubborn wall, listening and listening to words that are not meant for you.

You think: I've done wrong. You've brought disappointment and worry to your grandmother. You hate this. She has done so much for you. Your knuckles throb. They lock and sing red and ache from hitting Jacob enough times this morning to bust open his mouth, open like a jar of a thousand flies, the whole thick, wet swarm of them left to hang in the air and fall. Jacob with his big mouth spitting disrespect at everyone—*stupid bitch, faggot, dumb ho*—and today, this morning, after math class, because you stood in his way, he chose you.

"I'm afraid he'll end up in prison. On drugs. Or dead," she moans, gripping Becky's hand, the spare flesh over her knuckles shivering.

Next to a spoon, a plate of crumbs and salt, and on the plate, the shadow of the women's heads.

Your own throat flares.

The demon is taking Saint Michael's sword.

You eat the part of you that wanted to cry.

You should not be listening to any of this.

You bite your lip and hold your fists to your belly, unclenching them, quelling them, calling them home.

If only you, too, owned a saber to defeat the beast you fear.

Like a pane in the window of her worries, your grandmother's words have all cracked and shattered. "I'm just afraid," she mutters. "Abram needs to learn how to be a man. I'm thinking to ask Claudio back into the house to live."

"No. Oh, no. Don't. Don't say that." Becky puts her hand on your grandmother's shoulder because the bird of your grandmother's face has sunken into the soft earth of her hands. "You are being good to him. He has your goodness, Gertrudis. You're a part of him, always. Abraham has you to follow. God knows."

The part of you that loves your grandmother more than anything else rises up in your throat and sits there like a hard lump. On the wall across from where you stand, there is a mirror, and if you cock your head just right, you can see them: your grandmother, her friend, the plates, the mugs and the forks, benign shadows.

Uncle Claudio, you think, hearing your grandmother weep, seeing Becky console her. You remember the last time he came, the day after Christmas last year, how he threw food all over the table and the walls and kicked the TV, yelled at your grandmother and burst through the front door. He shouldn't come back, you said then and say to yourself again.

"He's my son. He's not all bad," your grandmother tells Becky. "I can't teach Abram how to be a man. But Claudio can. I think he can."

"No. This won't end good. I know he's your son, but, babe, that don't make him good."

"Don't start. Don't. I have enough to worry about . . ."

But Becky just shakes her head, and she holds your grandmother and pulls her close to her heart and kisses her hair. When you hear the squeal of the chairs, you know it is time for you to get back into bed. Still, you press your nose to the wall, and with Saint Michael next to your chin, you think of your father, digging far into the memories with nothing but the spoon of your want. When you return to your bed, you lay as quiet as a log.

It is November. The world is a cushion—flat and over-used, strangely dim and so far from its original form. You cross yourself, and the pecan limbs above the house gnash at the roof. Why would she invite him back? Am I really that bad?

Each night, you lay in this noisy little bed, fending off sleep, pushing it away like a hot sheet, watching the ceiling grow darker, watching the fan spin its life away, watching your hands glow with darkness and sometimes, if you're lucky, with light. Pushed against a wall, the old bed groans every time you move, and the fan across the room, perched on a chair, blows the hairs on your legs, falls on your cheeks like whispers and odd light or leaves that are fleeing. You wonder if these things that are wrong with your life might undo themselves: not suddenly or full of miracle, but slowly, loosening their grip enough so that with force, with want, with intent, you might someday, soon, slip away from them.

From your bed, the light from the hall is dim and slides beneath the door timidly. The voices from the kitchen have halted their work, and soon, you recognize the dim hum of Becky's truck engine. The headlights splay the darkness in the room, and the bed creaks, because you move to block the truck light with your pillow. As the light melts away, you wish you could shake off the thought of your grandmother worrying that you are lost, that the future before you is bleak and choked with troubles, filled with hardship, moving toward an irreparable ending.

Your eyes grow heavy. Leaden. Lint clogged. Smudged. Sludge.

She's made up her mind, you think. He's gonna come back.

The ceiling begins to fall.

The pecan tree scratches the roof.

Walls blur, then blaze in white, and then, with your head pressed deeply into the thin white pillow, your eyes grow heavy as clots. Though your eyelids sit on themselves, thick and demanding, though you do arithmetic and repeat dates, it comes.

You do not want sleep to come, but it does. Of course, it will. It always does.

The bed coils grunt.

2

Around you, the darkness is humming.

It vibrates. It eats up other, less potent noises, and when you awaken to it, shaken from a difficult dream, from a slight, shutterless sleep, one that was shallow and not made of comfort, the world is just the same, just as when you left it, and you accept this. What else can you do? You never can sleep through an entire night.

In the morning there is cotton in your mouth. You wait in bed, and the cold is on you like a fit. You grab at the blankets. And you don't want to get up.

In the other rooms, your grandmother moves stealthily, as quiet as dust.

The sink swallows water. The dishes clank with concern as they're rinsed.

Then, you listen to her footsteps. Soft steps. She brushes her teeth, spits. Flushes. She yawns. You can hear her lungs, or what you make of them, the launching of breath into the world as she sighs. The door shuts. You hear footsteps. And then, the light switch in the hallway.

For a very long time, you have not let your mind fix on your father. He wasn't a great man, not even a good man, but you know nothing about him, really, except that he died when you were three, and no one will tell you why or how. So you go along, like everyone else, like your grandmother and your uncle who never visits, just knowing, somewhere in the bald corners of your heart, that the space in the world he once filled is gone.

Sometimes you wish the whole world in front of you would stop. Pause for a second, a whole minute, even, and let you get off. What else would there be? Where'd you go? Who knows?

So you listen to your grandmother, the choreography of morning. You'll never understand why she does it, each morning the same. As you lay in bed, heavy eyed and listening, things swim to you: lightning and baseballs, eighteen-wheelers shrieking beneath the freeway overpass where you stand some afternoons and wish for a trip, for a sky full of eagles, for something bigger than paper airplanes and the cartoons you watched two years ago that made you laugh until your belly opened itself up like the mouth of a blue whale. It's what floods you at 4 or 5 or 6 a.m. You wonder if your grandmother endures a similar deluge of thoughts and memories and busies herself, then, necessarily, to keep them at bay.

The bed you are in is older than anything else in the house. It is hard and inflexible—the metal coils buried deep inside the old mattress gripe each time you shift, and it smells of other years, impatience. Unless you spray the fabric cleanser all over it, which is what you do some days, because the stitches of the fabric demand it to cover the odor of time, and this morning, as you muster up the will to get out of bed, the scent is ripe. This was your father's bed. Once. Years back. Before he was married to your mother. Before he died with your uncle nowhere to be found. Before your mother threw up her arms in despair and left.

You don't want sleep to come back.

You know you should get out of bed, start the day. But you lay there. You lay there and your knuckles are sore and you think and your body is open like a sigh, the lungs asking for air and time and hope.

Torcido. It's the word for what your grandmother fears. Twisted. Under the bucket of your tongue you say it a few times. It sits there. That word. An idea. It steams. You know what this means. *Torcido*. It smolders. The word that covers the mind in its milk, because you elude sleep, and every time you move, the metal yelps.

Although you don't know much about your father, you know this is the word your grandmother and her cruel sisters have used the two times you have overheard them discussing him. Not a good man, you have figured that much out. You know that he died and that no one mentions his name. You know you are not supposed to be like him.

Sometimes, you wonder if you are not supposed to hate him.

In biology class once, the teacher put three questions on the board. Sometimes when you are fighting off sleep, you can see those three questions amplifying their light, growing brighter, lit up with halogen or rancor, staring you down, each letter, each word increasing in size and weight and consequence and font.

Are babies born bad?

That was the question that screamed at you most.

You were supposed to agree or disagree.

"Is it possible, really, for the genes in our bodies to instruct us to be bad? To do bad things?" the teacher, with her pebble voice and hair like an oil spill, asked.

In class, seated by the window that overlooked the city, you imagined the millions of tiny cells in your body amassing in a mob, conspiring and chanting and propelling you toward fighting and hitting things, defending yourself and the ones you loved.

But the class quickly grew too loud, the brief discussion spinning beyond the teacher's control. Instead of the lab, instead of the lesson on the warrior gene, the teacher assigned bookwork, definitions and reading and note-taking, because, "If you guys can't behave during a warm-up, how will y'all act during a lab?"

By the time your grandmother calls you for breakfast, you've defeated sleep, pushing it away from your body like a plate of food you don't want. You think of the warrior gene ticking inside you, if it's there, if the past parts of your father are there, too, and you are grateful for every good thing your grandmother is—the food and *cariños*, the roof over your head, the fact that she still believes, even if only a little bit, that you can do this.

When your grandmother knocks on your door, she says, "*Ven*. Come eat."

You stir.

"Abram, get up. You can't go to school today, but Becky is coming to take you to get your hair cut, and then you can help her do the yard."

It's unlike your grandmother to slam any door, and though she doesn't slam your door when she orders you up, she shuts it firmly, maybe in frustration, and now you know that something is different.

You kick off the bedsheets, wadding them up at the bottom of the bed with your toes.

"*¡Ya voy!*" you yell. I'm coming.

∾ ∾ ∾

The street on which your grandmother lives is quiet, although, from time to time, a car will screech by with its loud bass or its sad accordions rattling the glass. Beside your room, a mighty pecan takes its long fingers and scrapes the roof. You are accustomed to this scratching.

Enough times, a day has wrapped around you like a fist, bandaged, taut and stiff, and enough times you have resisted the sleep that settles over you like a burdensome mist. You think of your father, and Becky waits for you to put on your shoes. You wonder if there is anything in the world you can do, or if it's true that some people are really just born bad, born to enact badness, born to punch and kick and scream and fight and destroy shit, because the genes in your body have selected you for it.

Perhaps this was true for your father.

Perhaps this is true for your uncle, with his slick ways and his fat police sheet, his visits that usually end in conflict, a stream of tears left staining your grandmother's cheeks.

With the darkness around you, you lay very still, the heavy animal of sleep dragging its fur over your eyes, and you fear that perhaps this may also be true for you: a hole in the ground. One in your head. A hole in the very middle of the heart. Another hole breaching the lungs, making them split.

Too many times your Uncle Claudio has done your grandmother wrong. But he's coming back, and sometimes, you just wish you had a good dad. And a mom. And a house in the north side of the city with three cars and family barbecues and Netflix nights, board games and a swimming pool . . .

∾ ∾ ∾

That morning, you're sitting in the chair at Fonseca's Cuts when you hear Becky say it.

Chonch is doing your fade, and the subzero blade is full of your stubble, so Chonch bangs the clippers, and the black fuzz falls to the floor, cascades, slow-motion-like and all of it happening because Becky has said your uncle's coming back and she doesn't want him there.

"No way," Becky admits, telling Chonch because maybe Chonch knows about this kind of trouble, because maybe Chonch and Becky know what it's like, the hard knocks of the world, the way things go bad, the true things about digging oneself a hole, then digging oneself out with your own teeth and your hands.

"I love Trudy, you know. Love her with everything I am, but this is bad."

"Maybe he needs to learn the hard way," Chonch says, looking you deadeye in the mirror. "Maybe he needs life to knock the shit outta him a couple of times. Maybe that's how he'll learn." Chonch presses the clippers hard against your scalp, near your ear.

You don't want Chonch to see your eyes. So you duck your head and just listen.

The light from the room gleams when it hits Chonch's hair, which is smoothed back and dark. "Some of us need to take it the hard way," Chonch adds and splashes your scalp with the green aftershave that burns. "Some of us make it out better, stronger."

With one knuckle, Chonch pries your chin upward, so that you have no choice but to look straight into the mirror, straight ahead into Chonch's stare. "Some of us, well, you know how it goes. Some go the hard way, and that's all she wrote. Another one bites the dust. *Se acabó.*"

As talc soothes the places where the blade took hair from your neck, the thought of the end sinks in. You don't want to die. You don't want a bad life. You don't want to walk any hard path.

Chonch's knuckles are hot when they graze your neck to untie the smock.

Se acabó. It ends. It ends. It ends.

You hear it again and again and again. All morning, the blade buzzes in your head.

3

"You see stars," you tell Ophelia, the really smart girl with the long red hair sitting next to you in front of the school on the morning of the day they let you come back. "The very first time. Not really stars, like from a bulletin board, all perfect, but like if stars were smaller, real small, like flies. Moving around. A herd of them."

Because she wants to know what it's like. What it feels like the first time you take a fist. Under the mesquite tree in front of the school, its arm low and bending, reaching upward and across the lawn and toward you, you hold her hand before the first bell rings.

She looks at your pale red knuckles and wants to know why you do it.

Her hand is soft. In your hand she is something you don't fully grasp, a softness you won't understand for the rest of your life.

"What's the point?" Ophelia asks. She pops a wedge of waffle into her mouth and chews. "You get kicked out of school. Nobody wins."

When a fist finds its mark on your body, what happens in your face, in the pink mass of cheek muscle or the round fibers of the chin, is much like a fire, like maybe the marvelous moment when the sun was first born, and its redness rises up like a hurt only another sun might be able to understand. How can you make words to show this? For one whole moment, for that long of an eternity, all the muscles of your body go limp—and there is clarity and noise and fire. Then, then, they swarm, the muscles, with a heat unbeknownst to anyone else. What happens next is hard for you to explain.

And so you are silent.

You nod.

You clasp her hand as if it was a feather or made of eggshell.

No words emerge from your mouth, which has parted like a bird letting its wings feel open and light and holy with sun. Buses line up, and you watch students exit them in orderly queues, like ants trekking across the pavement. Everything around you is bright. Methodically, the ants pass by, their notebooks and tattered backpacks and earbuds streaming in quick motion.

Nearby, a whistle busts the crispness in the air.

"I don't think you should fight anymore," Ophelia insists and offers you a piece of her waffle. Her hand is a bird, one made in autumn, dark and wonderful, coated— a promise of things soon to be.

Tiredness draws on your eyes, because you do not sleep very much or well. You stare at her hands and then at the trees at the far part of the schoolyard. The branches rise up from trunks like so many paths a living thing might follow.

"This will end badly," she says. Her voice has grown as thin as a leaf. "If you keep fighting . . . Nothing good can come from this, Abraham."

The way her head shakes disapprovingly puts a splinter in your throat.

Ophelia squeezes your hand. Her smile dwells on her face flatly, a mile of unquiet.

Is this an ultimatum? If you don't do what she says, then she's done?

"You don't understand." It's not enough to budge her. Staring at the ground, your eyes blink. They grow fat, burdened.

But her voice is no longer a leaf.

From the shame that you feel for not being how she wishes you to be, your eyes squat. You stare at the ground, and you tell yourself: Be hard. Don't say anything mean. Let her talk.

Because you're still holding her hand. And your hand trembles like something weak and unrooted. You fear the warmth in your palm will reveal itself and that she'll retract, pull back, run off into the sun.

"Fighting? Abraham, just stop."

It isn't as easy as that, you want to say.

I can't explain it, you wish you could utter.

It's how I protect myself. It's part of who I am, you could tell her.

But it sticks in the hollowest part of your throat. You wish you could just take her hand and put it behind your eyes or deep into your brain and say, See. Look. This is what it's like.

The warmth she would see. The taste of ideas. The little animal and the tangled strings of your DNA, the noises she'd hear . . .

There in the courtyard, the school day imposing its heaviness, her hand in yours, you want to crack open your ribs and show her the fat or thin whispers of your heart. Let Ophelia see you for all that you are, that sometimes you can't control what you feel, like now, or then, when you stare at her hair, which is red like a maple in the loveliest days of autumn, as its leaves say adieu to the limbs and journey into fate, into dissolution, into the dampness of the solid earth that awaits. When you stare at her eyes, you feel it, too, the warmth, for her eyes are dark like belonging and simple like all the words you know and the ones you still don't.

"It's hard," you say, finally. "Maybe one day I will find a way to tell you why." It's all you can create from the parts of your life that you don't yet know how to explain.

"Does it hurt?" she asks.

Her hand leaps to your shoulder. Slowly. Tenderness, soundlessness.

In her eyes sometimes the brown speckles turn green. You see that her hand also trembles, each of her fingers like reeds trembling in the wind.

You nod.

"What does it feel like? To get hit?"

"I can't say. I'll have to think."

The bell rings. Students make their way to the school doors. A teacher with a bullhorn waves to Ophelia.

"Move it! Let's go!" you can hear an administrator begin to holler.

Your ankle quivers, and your legs begin to shake.

Ophelia sees this. Trembling. Weakness. A part of you wants to stuff it down inside. You turn it off and cast it away, so that you won't feel embarrassed, so that she'll never see you weaker or less than sturdy.

"It's okay." She nods. And she holds your hand. "Tell me later, then." She smiles.

The sun has lifted itself into the sky. You walk toward the doors, bodies shuffling past you hurriedly. Later, years later, Ophelia will confess that for a while she thought she might actually save you; however, how wrong that is, the want to save a man, as if he were some wounded, imperiled dog, as if anyone else might have saved you if not yourself.

"Do your work," she tells you. "Be good."

The teachers begin to clear their throats, and the hallways swell. In the distance, you hear the clatter of onlookers as you stand in the very middle of the hall and reach into Ophelia, holding her, your arms wrapping around her fondly, like bold, fortunate ropes. "Like a truck. A Mack truck hitting a wall. That's what it feels like," you mutter, and you wonder if perhaps you're holding her longer and maybe even tighter than you should.

As they course by, the cheerleaders pause, their pom-poms hissing. A trickle of students trudge through the halls, around you, like slow, tall birds, and some like starships zooming into other dimensions—everything spins, especially your heart.

Especially your heart.

You text Ophelia. As she parts ways with you and heads up the stairs, behind her the length of her hair summons you.

walk home after school?

text me. if you get bored.

For the rest of the morning and even after lunch you will smell her sweetness cling to your shirt. It's gardenia and mint and a shampoo whose name you will never remember, but God, it smells good. For a moment, the world is perfect, and it is yours. And one day, far from now, when the whole world as you know it has changed, she will think of you one afternoon, with fondness, with a simple and genuine sadness, the kind of noise that rivals sand dunes and quagmires of mud and entire forests of fallen trees, and she will write, *This is what I always loved about him. "Can I walk you home?"* And she will mean it.

4

Your grandmother's laughter. From deep inside, a fountain-like dribble at first, a spurt like a waterwheel that soon, suddenly, erupts into huge, spewing laughter. You never thought you'd hear it. Not like this. Like a ribbon of birds emerging from a marvelous grove of cypress trees. You wake to the sound of her joy, the smell of bacon and hot coffee. It's Saturday morning, and there's a newspaper on the table in which your Uncle Claudio has buried his face.

"Abraham. Good to see you," he spits, rustling the paper. His eyes course over the edge of the gray sheet.

"He's looking for a job," your grandmother informs you, pointing proudly at your uncle with his face covered in words.

As you make your way across the room to your grandmother, who is busying herself at the sink, you think this scene is imagined and unreal. Are you dreaming? Snagged in some alternate version of how things might be?

Beneath your feet, the floor is luminescent, cold underneath your sockless soles and your toes. In her grip your grandmother holds a yellow dishrag, and when she hugs you, her hands smell of lemon rind and Comet.

"Amá. Leave it there. I'll clean," your uncle grunts, chewing sloppily. "My turn," he says, turning to you, his grin sharp over the goatee peppered with crumbs. From behind the newspaper his knuckles jut out. Rough, worn. You've seen them before, these proven parts of a man's body that have gone through things—walls and doors, faces and ribs.

Leaning back in his chair, your uncle, in his gray sweats and his undershirt, opens himself to you for a hug, arms stretched like two giant tongs. His arms are covered in tattoos. Intricate black and gray swirls, women in bikinis, sporting magnificent Aztec headdresses, watchtowers and proud peacocks with their splendid tail feathers and webs. Before you step into him, before the arms pull you in. Smeared with gray, his thumbs press into your back and cause it to fold. From his neck bone a rosary dangles in the ink of his chest. He hugs you and leaves his dark thumb smudges on your neck and shirt, and something inside the folded parts of your heart stifles itself, halts its motions and dents.

Pulled back, the kitchen's red curtains show the sky, which is gray and hard and without light, behind the behemoth pecans, behind your grandmother shaking off her wet hands and her face aglow with an unremitting lunge into today and the next and the way she wished, faithfully and with will, the rest of life would be.

The pot on the stove whistles.

The water in the sink sings.

The kitchen is yellow.

The heart inside you is yellow, then, too.

And when your uncle touches you, everything comes to an abrupt stop. For the entirety of a moment it does—you hear the earth and the voice of your bones, and you walk slowly out of your uncle, toward the sink. The kitchen, how it will mark your mind, just like this: A tender downcast square of a room, idled, snared. The room standing as still as an arm bone, one left to bleach in an open field under a heavyweight sun or in a dead creek with its cumbersome limestone. This kitchen, with its white little stove of blue gas flowerets and its low popcorn ceiling, its awkward Formica table that glares too harshly without a tablecloth, that never stands upright or balanced unless paper is folded into a fat square and shoved beneath the table's unwieldy leg. At night, the sparse light of the little room emerges from a simple bulb, but by day, like now, over the cluttered countertop, during the long hours, through the long, wide window above the white sink—the sun sneaks in, just a nettle, a thin ray, maybe, but enough to shed light on the cooking, the eating, the rinsing, the people waiting—these are the echoes you'll remember, these friends.

"I made eggs and *papas*," your grandmother tells you, and this brings you back. A glass dish on the table holds the mix, covered by a green towel neatly tucked into the bowl's white rim.

When your uncle pulls your body to him, you stand very still, because his arms feel like ropes. Both knotted and smooth at once, they are large, like missiles, and as they squeeze you, your lungs struggle for air so that you cough.

"Come on, now. I heard you were tough," he jeers, gripping your shoulder tightly. The words come out of a place in his mouth that no one can see.

You cough, and the cough sits in the air like a duck that has forgotten how to fly. It falters, zags, dives . . .

At the table, your grandmother joins two tortillas for you. Smeared with yolk, her plate is piled on top of Claudio's. She wears her hair in a modest gray braid, a long tail of neatness that parallels her spine. Her pills rattle against a blue saucer as she sets them on the table near her coffee. They have already eaten.

"Don't you want to eat?" she asks.

She is smiling, and you ask yourself, Is this real?

"So Grandma tells me you're in high school. A junior. How you like high school?"

"It's okay."

"Just okay? You play any sports? Got a girlfriend?"

"I used to play football. But I had to get out."

Your grandmother reaches over, rubs your arm.

Your eyes are pennies.

"So why no chick? You got my blood, so I know you good with the ladies." When he smirks, his teeth glint. A smirk like a rut etched in plywood.

And you loathe that he uses the word "chick." You hate that your blood is his, the sameness coursing through you like pinpricks of words entering the ear, becoming the air, the sigh, the wickedness of rage and ire and disgust for all the shit he's done poised to become the whole body. His blood, your blood.

"No." Firm, blocklike, your answer jars him. Your spine tightens. Your jaw clamps. Instead of joy that your uncle is here, you feel stuck and powerless to stop it. It has already happened, and now what will you do?

"But there's that one girl, no?" your grandmother, sipping her coffee, interrupts. Her voice like a hand smoothing out a bedsheet. "What is her name? Ophelia."

"Oh yeah? Tell me about her. This Ophelia. She fine?" As he speaks, he smacks, and the sound of saliva and tongue and tooth vexes you.

"She's not my girlfriend."

Why did your grandmother have to say this?

"Not yet," your uncle breaks in, grunting his laughter.

You wish. You wish you could smack the smirk off his jaw.

All of this happening outside of you is happening inside, too. Insistently, the heat that has overwhelmed you in the past begins to churn, and you wish you could lift him up by his neck and hurl him out of this house. Hurl him so hard he would land in Saint Petersburg or Anchorage with the other wolves or in the middle of the ocean, on an iceberg, maybe, alone and far, far from you and your grandmother and Becky and Ophelia, far from this little kitchen with its soft, lame light, its imperfect table and its four stove flowerets.

But you can't. And he rips off another piece of sweet bread and swigs from his mug. Crumbs spatter across the table, fall to the floor. He chews sloppily, and the table legs wobble.

"I'm gonna show you some things," he asserts, chewing and chewing and smacking his stout lips. "Things are gonna change around here, little boy." His mouth is as big as a continent.

∽ ∽ ∽

"I asked him to come. Abram, he's here to help," your grandmother tells you when you are alone on the back porch.

"Here to help?" you ask. Disbelief peppers your mouth.

The planks beneath where you sit are weathered with a woe known only by wood. Sparse grasses and a few empty pots, the plants within them long dead, litter the ground by the drooping steps. Somewhere, a dog barks, and you wish you had one, a dog.

The idea of your uncle doing anything other than screwing things up confounds you. Stirs inside your brain like a long metal rod, the kind used for swirling cement in a bucket, the kind you watched Becky use when she stabilized this once-crooked porch by digging three deep holes in the ground, inserting posts to bolster up the porch planks, then filling the holes with poured cement. "Just watch. You might learn something today," Becky told you, firmness and affection in her eyes.

"I don't think he should be here. Becky says it, too," you tell your grandmother on the now-steady back porch that overlooks pecan trees and neighboring roofs. But you pause as the words fall from your mouth, because you realize you only acquired this information by eavesdropping on their late-night talk, from listening to Becky and Chonch, and so you shouldn't have known this or said it. "I mean, I bet if you asked her, Becky would say no. I know she would."

Your grandmother strokes your hair. Her hands, two sad nets.

In the patches of grass and dirt, the pecan trees stand motionless. Their last leaves still clinging to limbs, rebelling or unable or even, maybe, eager but not exactly ready to fall. A squirrel scampers around the downed leaves, which crackle each time the creature hops. A plane somewhere in the sky takes hundreds of people to the next part of their lives. You look upward, but nothing. Only the sound.

"Give him a chance, Abram."

～ ～ ～

An hour later, in front of the mirror that stands in the hallway, near the bath, near the closet with the old folded towels and the blankets for winter, near Saint Michael holding guard over the demon on the wall, you find yourself. In the mirror, you look twice your size. You take out bedsheets and a blanket for your grandmother to wash—these will be for your uncle—and behind you, as quiet as a moth, your grandmother sweeps.

You stare at your hands, two huge spoons attached to the long bones of the arms.

You are standing in front of a mirror, and your eyes flicker, a blinking that does not settle when you command it to. Your neck is a rod that holds up your head, its only job, its dutiful obedience to keep you looking ahead. And your jaw has widened, your body has thickened, your arms are much larger than you ever thought they'd grow. These days to come, the life you are making versus the one that has been made for you, for you, a man, excites you.

Your hair is the color of Saint Michael's boots, the hilt of his sword, too.

Inside your shorts, your parts struggle to breathe.

Now, your grandmother has to tiptoe and reach high to put her thumbs on your scalp. The broom stands against the wall. In the middle of the hall a dust pile waits to be lifted. It wasn't long ago that the two of you were the same height. It wasn't long ago that you said, One day I'm going to be an astronaut and I'm going to walk on Mars. Now, you're not so sure. Not of anything aside from the simple facts of your life: that you love your grandmother, that November is when the pecans fall to the ground, that Ophelia is smart and kind and beautiful, that you want a dog and somehow, maybe because you'll be stronger, or maybe because you'll read it in a book or watch a movie that will inspire you to do it or maybe because one day you'll just wake up and everything will work itself out, somehow, somehow, you will leave your fists behind. A simple fact—determination and so much at stake—that you're afraid of what you'll become, that you don't think your uncle belongs, that you will become just like him. The worries flank you. It might have been easier becoming an astronaut.

Vividly, you recall when you were smaller and, crossing a parking lot, your grandmother holding your hand, nights when she'd make popcorn and you'd chomp pickles, cheering on the Spurs, or those difficult nights after your mother left, when your grandmother sat by your bedside each night, the bed squeaky and imbalanced, and recited prayers, because this, she claimed—instructing you to brace your hands together in a small teepee—was the way to calm your spirit, the way to ask God to look after your mother, the way to help yourself summon sleep. Later, older, you wondered why your grandmother never guided you to pray for your mother to come back.

In the mirror, in the hallway, in the tiny wooden house in the middle of this incredible world, with Saint Michael wielding his blade as vigilant as an owl and your uncle in the other room, the television louder than it knew it could ever speak, with the pecan trees loving their last few days with their leaves, perhaps, indeed, you might wield the world in your hands, make the best of what you've been given. But this is a lifetime away, an uncertain span of variables and a trumpeting of disquiet, while your uncle, it seems, is here to stay.

"He's going to make things better, Abram." Your grandmother smiles.

In front of the closet, your grandmother holds your hand. You feel the sound of her heart, that heat, that solid rhythm, untangled, tangible somehow, threads and ribbons, fibers, veins, twine and vines. The idle trees through the little window in the kitchen grow dark, and you detect this through the glass. Then you wish for some wind and wonder if trees ever did the same.

"But he can't help us, not if you don't let him," she adds.

∾ ∾ ∾

That evening, your uncle sits in front of the TV and bounces his bull of a voice off the walls: "Grab your shit, Papo. I'm taking you to work out."

It's a dense voice, full of accidents.

You were cleaning your shoes, whitening them, and loathing saturates your bones when he calls you Papo. It's not your name, not even close. And you'll never know why he does it. A joke, perhaps, some other idiosyncratic tic.

In the car, on the long freeway, your Uncle Claudio tells you about free weights and how to put on size, become stronger—tuna and tortillas, dumbbells, chicken meat, 45s and milk—and you think, Damn, this guy might be wise after all. The real deal.

While he drives, he is calm, his knuckles gripping the wheel firmly. His own arms are built well, and so you listen, like listening to a dentist when you want better teeth. Meanwhile, the voice inside you continues to wish him gone, though you wonder if this is what he's really like. Knowledgeable. Giving. So willing to share what he knows. Both hands on the wheel. His voice as thick as a log. Sturdy. Like maybe this part of him was lost and now that he's found it, he is able, finally, to come home. But how do you know when you can believe someone's words? You aren't sure.

"We have to find something for you, Abraham. Something for you to be good at. Damn good at," your uncle says, his chin stoic and stern, and you hope one day, for a moment, you hope that your face will grow this way, stout and full of itself and strong. He keeps nodding. You hope one day you will know shit, like he does, that people will sit beside you and listen with their ears wide open and the whole world flashing before them. The socks on his feet are white like bone. Around the steering wheel, his knuckles pop out as if someone has placed bolts underneath the skin of his hands. "Something that one day can make *us* some money."

You listen. *Us.* You listen, and inside you a shred of belief has fattened itself up like a small, thick snail growing too wide for its shell. When did we become *us*?

Before you can reach the gym, before you can take this new plan for your life out of its box, take it for a test run, his phone rings, and he swings into a parking lot, because there is a more pressing matter for your uncle with both hands on the wheel and his socks as white as bone to deal with.

"Tomorrow," he tells you, dropping you off in front of your grandmother's house. "We'll hit it tomorrow." Something's come up. His voice tails off like a kite.

5

It's the second quarter, and the Cowboys are losing terribly. On the television a commentator laments the loss of an era, how a team can slide into mediocrity and what an organization might do to ascend from these depths. In the bald commentator's hand, the microphone shimmers, waxy and undeterred, and the green turf behind the speaker is greener than any green you've seen spurting out of the ground. The man's tie is red. He mouths his words like each one of them had the meaning of every true thing in the world.

In the living room, your feet tuck beneath you, sockless and cold, and outside, the wind bulges. Ordinarily this room seems small and comfortable and squat, but with your uncle around, it seems larger somehow, like the house has had to expand in order for him to fit. On the sofa beside you is your grandmother, her hands like two birds, small and patient, pressed together in her lap. Beside her is the small space heater with its orange heart flaring for everyone to see. She watches the Cowboys and dozes off, waking up from time to time as if bothered by sleep itself.

"Who's winning?" your grandmother mumbles, the sleep on her like a coat.

In the recliner, his legs up, your uncle shutters his eyes, the remote perched on his chest.

Life, you think. This is what I have to look forward to. The commercial for beer, the pizza commercial, the new Toyota commercial, the commercials for shaving cream and deodorant for rugged men. Cheerleaders shaking their pom-poms and their white, white boots.

"Let's do this!" your uncle proclaims suddenly, his voice a fiery cannonball slung across the room. The chair rocks from the force he produces getting up, and the remote flies across the floor.

"Do what?" you ask.

"What happened? What happened?" your grandmother slurs, trying haplessly to lift herself from her sleep.

"Grab your bag, Abramito. Your tennis shoes. Bring an extra shirt and shorts."

He leaps toward the kitchen.

"For?"

"The gym. I'm taking you with me to the gym."

"But the game's not over."

"Who's Jim?" your grandmother, in her half slumber, asks, clutching her heart with two shivering hands.

∽ ∽ ∽

That afternoon, your Uncle Claudio teaches you how to bench-press and explains how the muscles of the chest work and are complemented by the biceps and the triceps when you let the weight down and then have to extend your arms to propel it upward. With zeal, you listen, your eyes wide open.

"When you do this, press the weight upward, away from the body," he tells you. "It'll burn."

He's right, it does burn. The more repetitions you put in, the more times you push the resistance away, the more it burns. This is a good thing, because the muscles are tearing and soon, with good nourishment and sleep, they will rebuild, scarring themselves in layers, and this is how mass is built, how more difficult tasks are overcome.

"It's how you get bigger," he explains.

"Hey, don't let your elbows break ninety degrees," he instructs as you lower the bar with four fat plates just beneath your pecs. It is a slow descent. You think of math class, the drawings in your textbook of perfect right angles, and you obey.

"Now up." He steadies the bar, his two fingers below it. A fulcrum.

"A one hundred and eighty-five pounds. Damn, Papo! First day at the gym. Tha's what's up, Daddy."

He grins, and something inside you like a radio wave or a lantern cutting through darkness begins to beam, so you grin, too. It's a harness, this light, this noise, and it loosens you up, your disbelief, your worry, your desire for him to go.

Next he demonstrates how to do diamond push-ups and how you can turn these into Spider-Mans by kicking up your knees toward your elbows each time, to extend the triceps.

"You'll feel it. Here. And here," he tells you, pointing to the back side of your arms and then to the middle of your chest.

This is difficult. Like mallets are taking their turns at the bones. Your muscles ache, but you know this is useful, imperative, you know it is what is required to build strength. You want that, strength, more of it, mass and ability and form. So you give it your all, and you can see something in front of you, a light, maybe a tree, maybe a bird, which you've never seen before.

Next, you do butterflies, which means you will sit with your spine upright and make Ls with your arms, which are outstretched near your ears, and you pull the weight in, extending the flat outside muscles that form the perimeter of your chest so that the inner muscles squeeze. You do three sets of these butterflies and then end with the incline. And this one is fourth on your regimented list of chest tasks. Because the seat is positioned at a slant, you call it incline, and it works the top of your pectorals, which are the chest muscles. If you work them right and regularly, a valley will develop between your two pecs.

"You want this," your uncle says and points to his own swollen chest, which owns a deep-shaped slope between the two mounds of muscle. "You have to commit," he says, tapping the peak of his chest and pointing, posing in the long mirror.

The announcement in the mirror, the dialogue between the lights and your two bodies and the electricity of courage is like fuel you feel within the thin, slim vessels of your long veins, each pulse a reminder of what could be.

Huffing, sloped over from the exhaustion, watching him shine in the glass, you say, "Yes. Yes. I can do this. I want to come again."

In the car you tell him about fighting, because he asks, and he asks because your grandmother told him you've gotten in some trouble at school.

He says you should put this energy to good use.

He says good things are on their way. That good things come to those who don't sit around and wait.

He asks what you want to do with your life. Tells you the world is an oyster. It's yours. Crack it. Eat it up. And you know the rest.

That night, you want to thank him, to tell him everything about the rest of your life. But to take such a minute, to show that? Would he sit beside you, listen intently as you splayed your heart or yanked the true things inside your gut and displayed them like tripe? Would he know this, recognize his own troubles in yours and say, I've been there, Papo. You can do this. Do it better than I did.

After your shower, after eating the two cans of tuna he bought you, after brushing your teeth minty fresh and deflating your gym bag, you sit on the couch and wait, because his car is not in the driveway, and you don't know where he's gone, though you want him to come back. Funny how that works, isn't it? The television lights up the room with a soft fuzz. Already the muscles of your chest and arms have started their anguish. Not a scream, not yet. Not panic or yowling but soreness, enough of it to underscore that tomorrow is coming and there is more work to do.

November has fallen, and the world has gone gray and bold. The sun is falling out of the sky. After an hour, the Patriots are dominating the Bills, and you realize he's gone, that your uncle probably won't be back anytime soon, so you turn off the game and head to your room. The muscles in your chest sting. There is so much you want him to know.

The familiar vibration of your phone: *Just wanted to say good night.*

Ophelia, you whisper to yourself before you punch your head into the pillow and try not to fall asleep.

∾ ∾ ∾

"Like what, Claudio?" your grandmother asks over chicken and rice the next day, after your uncle tells her he has a plan. She brings over the coffeepot and pours more, white steam rising over the mug rim.

Beside your uncle you sit and watch your grandmother's eyes like two seeds beginning to break shell. Nervously, you wait for your uncle's words to careen from his mouth. At the old table with its cloth the color of watermelon hearts, your grandmother stirs a lump of sugar into her red cup. You imagine the little granules like oddly shaped fish disappearing into a dark lake. Like a swan, steam flutters above the cup.

One day you will remember this swan. Its silences, its noise.

One day it will be how you remember everything.

You will recall the old wooden table and the three oak chairs, the sound they make when the imperfect legs drag across the cold linoleum, like a happiness that lost its footing, trying something new each time to find it. You'll reminisce about the coldest Novembers, the trees losing each of their leaves, the little heaters with their orange hearts glowing throughout the house, the sun radiating whittled promises and pacts it makes with birds from high in the sky. You will remember the day your Uncle Claudio came home. His fistfuls of newspaper, his arms that were grayed by experience, by peacocks, *ganas*, pyramids and sacred hearts. Your grandmother's laughter, too. Filling her throat like a mountain of moths, then, filling the kitchen and all of the rooms, so much fluttering, so much wingspan. The fluttering that was hope. Each laugh with a set of its own bold wings. The day the whole world changed—the beginning, the middle and yes, of course, naturally, the end.

You will tell your first love all about her. About the swan. About your grandmother. About Becky and your uncle. About the little crooked table with its pantheon of tablecloths, so many different hues and prints, each fabric folded neatly into impeccable squares in the hall closet by the Saint Michael painting. About how everything, soon, not long after your uncle with his big hog hands and his mud voice came, as you'd feared, went horribly, irreparably wrong.

Sometimes, later, when there is hardness happening inside of you, when your face explodes into ten thousand splatters, when you don't know what to do next or what has happened or how you will ever resolve it, you will think of the swan, the soft chatter like an easy gravel falling onto a long road, unpaved, simple and difficult and necessary—a road all boys, or boys like you, must walk.

One day when you tell your girl about the swan, you will stand there by the cabinet where your grandmother keeps all the good pots and pans, the ones her sisters gave her the Christmas your grandfather died, long before you were made. This conversation with your girl will occur long after your grandmother has also died, six or seven years after that fact, and you will look at Ophelia, noting the stem-brown flecks of her eyes, like a field of bone grass or fallen pecan leaves, thinking of the sweetness that Ophelia carries, all jasmine and the eucalyptus of searching, recalling your grandmother toiling in the little room, her hands over the sink by which you and your love stand, washing dishes or putting away forks, the wrinkles of your Buela's hands wiping the counter with the lemon cleanser she liked, the yellow rag in her palm like a wrinkled petal from a strangled flower. Recalling the hard clangs and racket of the pots being moved after washing or before a meal, the big swan crossing paths again and the painting of Saint Michael overcoming your demon, you will say, "Yes, I miss her." At this point, your voice has whittled itself down to a twig, so thin that it's nothing and all of what you have. Your love will understand how this means you are alive, and she will hold you about the waist, and it will be the first time in many years that riots of hot tears will exit your eyes. "Yes, I love you," you will say to your love, whisper to her in the soft leaf of her neck, her heart entering you from behind. You are a memory, she will pull you to her, and the pulse that steps inside you is your song. You name the swan Maribel, and you think that's a lovely name for a white bird that is lighter than smoke.

At the little wooden table with its crooked legs, you watch your grandmother's coffee swirl as she hears your uncle's big plans for you and your fists. So many turns, so many little revolutions. You lose count of how many times the spoon circles. But by then, the sugar has all dissolved and your uncle is still telling his story.

"Like boxing, Mom. I'm thinking Abraham, I could get him into boxing. In no time, he could go pro. Pro, Papo. You hear what I'm saying? Big time. Cash, Daddy. I'm thinking today is the day."

You don't want to look up.

Your uncle's voice is shining, its own pilfered fuel hot and marvelous. His voice is larger than itself, greater than the greatest oaks, larger than the tower in the very center of your city. And you want it to stop.

"Yes!" Your grandmother has bitten the bait. She drops her mug onto the saucer. It clangs, and she praises God.

Your uncle glances at his phone. "Or tomorrow. We should jump on this tomorrow," he says, slurping a spoonful of meat and broth. The broth dribbles on his chin, and your grandmother hands him her napkin. "I gotta handle some stuff, but tomorrow. We start this. First day of the rest of our lives!"

His teeth are as big as stones, and at the table, beside him, your plate scraped bare, your teeth press into themselves. It is a friction you loathe. Your fists swell, and the swan is nowhere to be found. You stare at your grandmother's grin, a sweet, simple happiness, but you wish she'd take back her napkin and wipe it away. Wipe it off before it crumbles. You don't want him to see that a piece of you, a slim mote of care somewhere in the flat swamps of your gut, wants you to believe in him.

Your grandmother stares at you, anticipation in her eyes.

"Sounds good," you utter. Your arms arching, sore and bitter from the pressing, from the tears.

"Sounds good? Real damn good," he adds, lifting himself from the table, occupied by the screen of his phone.

Your voice tells you, Calm down. All the muscles around your heart begin to scream.

6

In the morning, while your grandmother gets ready for work, you stand in the hall and stare at your uncle, who has slept on the sofa, his shoes strewn across the rug.

"Shhhhh," she whispers. "Your uncle, he's asleep." With her chin, she points, her hands loaded with foil and spoons.

The house is quiet.

Three tacos wrapped in foil, which are warm in your palm as if they were alive and had heartbeats that gave heat and kindness and love. She hands them to you and kisses your temple. You place the tacos in your backpack, behind a book, a notebook and the homework you forgot to do.

It doesn't make sense. Looking at your uncle, his thickset chest rising, the soft eagle blanket from Mexico pulled over his forehead, you wonder why he isn't up, isn't helping, isn't with his eyes buried in a newspaper searching for work. Instead, he's asleep as your grandmother tiptoes around him, readying herself for work, leaving his tacos in the microwave.

You wonder what he did last night.

Your arms are sore, all the muscles of your chest, too. But your hands want to drop a glass or rattle the pans, flip on the TV or knock firmly on his skull. Anything. Purposefully. A reminder that this isn't the way it should be.

Something to make this right, even, level. So you try to conjure some other event to occupy your mind, some story or song or one of the Greek myths you are learning at school that can absorb your thoughts from the anger staring you down. But Icarus is not interesting today. And Medusa cannot turn this to stone. Nothing comes to mind.

A mute rain falls. The road shines. It is vague and soft and noiseless. You stand by the door. Your backpack tugs down on your shoulders, heavier now than you ever remember—books and notebook paper, your three tacos, your father and the steep, shivering fear that you will bend, ending up like him or your uncle, a bad man with a bad life, suffering and rage and destructiveness.

From the glass door, you watch your grandmother dart out to Becky's old red truck. She holds an egg-blue scarf over her hair and a clump of foil in her hands. She wears happiness and waves as she jumps into the open waiting door. The rain makes the whole world fuzzy.

Your phone buzzes: *Going to read you a letter.*

The sound of it places a small joy inside of you. So you sit at the edge of your bed and think of a box of letters. Ophelia's most valued possession. Once Ophelia told you about this box, these letters—from her mother—they were everything. Reading them, penning responses, holding them in the emptiness of her hands, the ones attached to her arms and the other pair, too, the hands that grew inside her heart, which allowed her to hold things and keep them.

Beneath her bed Ophelia keeps her stash of envelopes. Each one from Afghanistan. After she'd read one a dozen times, she'd place it in this box, reading it again when sadness or other afflictions sat on her shoulders like a pallet of bricks. Sometimes she'd just sit with the tin box of letters on her bed, beside her or perched on her belly, balanced there, as if holding them near her is enough to quell the fusillade occurring inside.

The rain subsides. But it falls still, slovenly, striking the weak glass in a slow patter. You wonder what it would be like to lay on the bed with Ophelia. Would it solve everything, anything at all? To hold her, to weave your fingers inside the lace of her fingers, and the sky, would it still be gray? Would she ever let you get that close?

When Ophelia texts, your bones breathe new life: *Aunt's truck won't start. Walk to school??*

"Yeah! Hell yeah!!" you want to respond, but instead, you hold your excitement like a pup that wiggles wildly, wanting to free himself from its tethers. Instead, you wait a couple of seconds, then reply: *Yup yup see you in ten.*

It takes less than that for you to run three streets over to Ophelia's aunt's house. Each stride, your backpack smacks your spine and threatens to tackle you from behind. You wear a bulky black hoodie, the cotton absorbing most of the raindrops, absorbing them, pulling them in, keeping them so that the fabric grows increasingly wet. Pummeling your back, the weight of the backpack is enough to crush you, to topple over every solid happening. Like a paddle, your heart beats in your throat, a long wooden oar slapping at water. The rain has died down. But still, the puddles jettison water upward, soaking your pant legs and shoes and socks, splashing you each time your foot strikes the sidewalk.

At the corner before Ophelia's house, you stop and catch your breath, which slips from you now in thrusts and hissing. In November, in the part of the world where you're from, the trees blacken, have lost nearly all of their leaves, and what's left are the dark sinews, the fat mired trunks that split off into a hundred besmirched limbs, not so heavy looking now as they jut into the sky.

Ophelia waits on the porch, thumbing through a book. You pull out the umbrella you've stashed in your bag, which is apple-orchard red, a single burst of color on this gray street with its leaflessness and wet worry and the puddles that grow larger with every breath of the dark clouds. It isn't a long walk to campus, but it's a good one, because it gives you time to talk.

"Thanks." She hugs you.

Because your hoodie is wet, she giggles, and her smile is a valise in which so much is held. You hold out the red umbrella, and she steps under it. As you walk, she reads to you.

So you walk slowly.

Some days you talk about school—teachers and fights and homework and things she read in English, her favorite subject—but other days, you walk in silence, the worlds inside each of you loud enough to fetter tongues.

Today, though, she reads to you. A letter from her mother. A letter about rain.

It's raining here at the base. Her voice ardent. You listen carefully enough, and you can hear its light. Each word emerges from her throat with purpose and fuel, glimmering, throwing its colors, coming together in awesome formations of meaning and delight and assemblies of thought, constellations of hunger and comfort.

Today she reads a letter about happiness and truth and rain.

M'ija, I am afraid sometimes that I have not told you how much I love you. I want you to know this. My love for you. To never forget it. Though I am far, the other side of the world, to be exact, remember this: I love you, Ophelia. I love you, my beautiful, beautiful girl.

You wonder why she reads these parts. The parts that name her. The parts that put sadness like a splinter in your wet heart, the heart wishing jealously, though you'd never confess it, that you, too, had someone to write you letters and tell you these parts. But instead, instead of passing over them, the parts about the love her mother holds for her, Ophelia puts them out for the trees and the long, cracked sidewalk and the darkness of the sky and the darkness inside you to hear—if these were your letters, you would skip over these parts, swallow them whole or leave them on the page. Never speak them to anyone at all, because, well, just because. But again, maybe you wouldn't even tell anyone you got letters, much less read them out loud or take them to school, or maybe you would, maybe you'd only tell Ophelia, because Ophelia is Ophelia and would understand the value of letters and mothers and true things about rain.

As she reads, Ophelia is unhurried, holding each page firmly, with care and tenderness in the tips of her fingers, with her eyelashes extending themselves deeply into the fibers of every paragraph, each syllable, every line made for her eyes, her thumbs gripping the soft pages' damp edges. Around you, the water falls.

So you hold the umbrella above your heads. You fear the ink will smear. You want nothing in the world to disturb her. Raindrops smack the soft pages, which are fragile and precious, and so you tip the red umbrella forward to shield Ophelia's letters, and this is how she reads, making sounds from the pen marks made on the other side of the world. She reads with you by her side, with the sky above her giving the world its smallest parts, with the taut red nylon deflecting rain and keeping things safe. Unfaltering, Ophelia walks, with her sunflower rain boots interrupting the flat gloss of the wide, imperfect sidewalk, the gloss that is water and chance and the reflection of the leafless trees, the grayest of mornings, her red, red hair, paper.

And so, I need you to love you, her mother wrote, and Ophelia reads. *I need you to look in the mirror each day and see goodness and to do goodness and to remember goodness, because there are enough bad people in the world, honey, bad people doing bad things, bad people who would eagerly steal that goodness, your goodness, and do God knows what with it. I need you to do this all of your life: know yourself, guard yourself, be true to yourself, love yourself, my good girl, my Ophelia.*

Be friendly, but do not trust that every man or woman is your friend, nor that each of your friends is as trustworthy as you. Love your friends, keep them safe and close to you, especially the ones who would do for you as you would do for them. Not everyone can do that, m'ija. Not everyone will. Not everyone is your friend. And that's okay. It really is. And yes, speak your mind, speak what you know to be true, but sometimes, many times, remember that some speech only requires you to listen. Know when to speak. Know when to battle. Know to think, yes, think, think, think always, before you send your true things into the world like birds, m'ija. When you are angry, especially, or remembering hurt or hurting, then, especially then, watch your tongue, hold it very near your heart, ensure that what you say is pure and necessary and from a place of love. Love the world, love its goodness, love that you are part of it. But most of all, more than anything else in the world, love you,

Ophelia. Love you. Nothing good can come from not lov-ing oneself. I know this. I have learned the hard way, and I write this so that you do not follow my errors, but so that you can do better and reach higher and have more, and should the day come that I am no longer living, remember that I have loved you like I love myself.

By the time you have reached the front of the school, Ophelia's throat is in a knot. Her fingers, delicate things, thin like twigs, gnarl and grip the letter tightly. None of this inflicts harm or discomfort, because the only thing you feel is warmth, a warmth no one in the world ever bothered to tell you about.

"I miss her," Ophelia says, standing in front of the school as rain pelts the world.

Her hair is redder than anything else.

Her mouth is a time and a place that you will return to later, unavoidably, for joy, for something marvelous to offset the heaviness of despair.

There is no sun to be found, and the clouds gather like dark geese, and they rumble.

She hugs you.

"I'm afraid, Abram. I want her to come home."

7

In front of your grandmother's little wooden house, the sun occupies the sky like an enormous yolk. Ophelia pats your knee as you sit on the front fender of your uncle's car. Her touch sends tremors down your leg. Puddles still polish the ground, and mud ruts dig into the earth, wide infractions, deep cuts. A few last brave leaves cling to the trees.

"She just didn't like my essay, I guess," Ophelia admits, swallowing her words like lumps of clay.

"Why?" you ask, unsure of what to say back to a girl as smart as Ophelia.

She is perched on the hood, her foot resting on the bumper, chrome and shiny, even in the fading fall light. Upset by her English teacher, Ophelia confesses, "I could have lied and written a different essay, and maybe she would have liked my lie and maybe, then, I would have a good grade."

"What was the topic?"

But before she can respond, your uncle sticks his bald head out the door and yells, "Get your ass off my car!"

His voice is brutish. Rust clad and gruff, thick like chain.

You help her down.

"Thank you," she whispers, her mouth halved like an apple.

You wait.

Blushing a deep red from the rebuke, she continues hesitantly. "I haven't heard from my mom. It's been awhile. No letters."

The blood in your throat crusts and takes on the weight of her sadness. It makes your throat grow fat with words you want to say.

This was the reason she'd taken the letters to school. In English class, they were to write an argument about whether fear was beneficial or if it hindered, and Ophelia took the letter to prove that fear impedes and harms and binds us. She tells you this as you walk to your grandmother's wooden porch, the last shards of sun reflecting on her hair, your uncle's voice forgotten now and minuscule.

"You think she's okay?" you ask, knowing well it's the wrong thing to say, but what else can you say? Isn't silence worse?

Often you've wondered about her mother. What life must be like for her. So far from home. In a war zone. Living so near dying. So far from Ophelia.

Perhaps the trouble with the essay isn't the real matter. Ophelia took the advanced English class, the harder one, the one where you read more and have to write essays instead of doing so many work sheets, the one she encouraged you to take if you were even partly serious about doing something great with your life. But the piece she just shared about her mom not writing, it is everything you knew that she fears.

"I hate war. I hate it," Ophelia mumbles, tears in her eyes.

You wish, at that moment, like so many other instances dragged across time, that you could wield that fire, the fire of her fear in your hands, grip it fully and yank it out of her, maybe vanquish it far from her sight, so that it never plagues her again. Perhaps you can. Perhaps you can allow her to pass it onto you, this fear, to permit you to ball it up in your hands and make it so small, so manageable, and take it into yourself, bury it deeply in the rut you already carry in your gut.

"Do you think . . . ?" you begin and then hold the thought.

"My family will eat dinner together every night," Ophelia continues as you sit down on your grandmother's porch step, the wood cold.

You nod. You always nod whenever she talks.

"I like that idea."

You smile, because her ideas are so grand sometimes, like hot-air balloons rising vividly and with joy over the horizon. So colorful. Vibrant and courageous against the city land. Showing gravity another way to live.

But then Ophelia says nothing, her teeth pressed tightly into the plum that her lips form.

How quickly the conversation has died.

How quickly the nerves have set fire to themselves.

On the porch step, you hold her hand again. The wood creaks beneath you. At first, she minds it, shifting her palm away irritably into her other palm, and holds it there motionless.

"You know, sometimes my aunt just sits at the table on Facebook," she says. "She won't say a word to me. She'll eat a little bit, like pick at her food, but she'll text and laugh to herself and go through photos. My mother says this is the curse. Having so many devices is bad luck. I hate the sound of a fork hitting somebody's teeth."

"Why does she do that?"

"It's not all bad. Technology, I mean," Ophelia clarifies.

She grabs at your hand then. Clutches it in her palm like a small animal she's found in the dirt. The pace of her chest generates its own small heat, a soft mound of the earth starting on its own to move. The little gold cross sitting below her neck glimmers, rising and falling just above her chest. You both sit on your grandmother's porch, the puddles giving the sky back its light, a siren singing its fire song streets away.

"I should get back," Ophelia announces. "It's Monday . . . my mom might Skype. I need to be there. In case."

And you nod, knowing this is one thing the two of you share—missing parents. Ophelia hasn't told you much about her dad, except that he left with another woman when she was five and that now he has his own family, a new one, with kids and a wife and a house in Dallas. Her mother, an army medic, was sent to Afghanistan last year. Although it isn't the same—not having one's parents around—it's close enough to what you're familiar with to give you a bond.

Some nights, when you sit with your thoughts, you imagine Ophelia also sitting in a dark room alone with only a lamp and the computer monitor giving her light. She waits and waits and hopes to see her mother's face materialize from the other side of the world.

"I'm sure she's just busy. Hard to write when you're saving the world."

Ophelia produces a half grin, her teeth pearly and perfectly imperfect. She clutches your hands, both of them. You love this.

Above you, the wind ruffles the trees, and the pecan runs its long limbs over the roof. Somewhere in the neighborhood the noise of a fire truck and dogs howling occupies the sky. For a second, the weight of the world is as light as a pin. For the rest of time, you will consider Ophelia's smile and this moment of you holding hands on your grandmother's porch in November.

Gradually, the world around you is losing its heat, the sun's departure forging pink and orange flares on the horizon. The light peeks through the tree branches, filtering the pink and orange rays. You stare at Ophelia's hair. The color of sunsets and cinnamon. Behind the sharp, dark tips of the trees the sky is emblazoned, and for a few minutes Ophelia sits beside you, your hands woven together, the simplest form of communication. Ophelia kicks a mud chip from her boot, and together you watch it rile up a puddle. The ripples. You listen to her breathe, and when her head falls onto your shoulder like a warm shadow, you understand, then, that you could have lived every day of your life like this.

While the world is getting colder, you think about asking her if she needs a blanket. Instead, you take off your hoodie and place it on her legs.

"Here," you say, covering her skin, "let me walk you home."

8

Fathom.

It's one of the nine words the teacher writes on the board for your English class to define. Beside *reparation, solace, pungency, idol.* The letters pop off the whiteboard like insect parts, spider legs and thorax fibers, antennae and butterfly bones. When you define these vocabulary words, you're supposed to write down what the term means in your own words, of course. Then you give an example of the word in a sentence and then a nonexample, or what it does not mean, and finally you draw a picture to show you've learned it.

Fathom. It means to imagine something. That's how you paraphrase it. Your example sentence: *I can't fathom why my grandma's girlfriend would help my loser uncle get a job at her factory.*

It's the truth.

Becky helped him, and you don't understand why. But she vouched for your uncle, and he got a job inventorying trucks parts for Tundras, and each evening, while the house you're in shushes itself to sleep, he carries the lunch your grandmother has prepared for him, he checks to make sure he's packed his headphones, he steps into the cusp of darkness, down the crooked wooden steps, and starts his car. Like a lion, the engine roars. The house is quiet when he's gone. You enjoy his absence.

He's a man. And you don't know many men, not men like him, men with consuming appetites and worries and grins that stir discomfort and anger inside you, rude men, men without manners or boundaries, men who carry fistfuls of power and hunger and aggression as if these were suitcases, as if these were hogs taking men to slaughter. But another place in your body is full of him, convinced he belongs, that he has goodness to lay on the table like a feast for a sad boy like you, one with his own worries, his own suitcases, his own hungers for life.

The truth is you wanted. You wanted life. Wanted him or someone to show you what it all meant, what it could be, what it took.

Who doesn't want when he's seventeen?

When you've looked in the mirror, the face in front of you is the face that hangs in the hall, the photo your grandmother has kept of her two sons, arm in arm, their clothes neat and firm and the soft sun like felt pulled gently over their bodies. In front of your grandfather's old Chevy, they stood and beamed, and your grandmother has treasured this photograph over all others. It hangs in the hallway, and sometimes, when you walk by it, you turn your face or look down, but other times, other times, you stare full on and study their bodies, their postures, their neat-creased khakis, their undershirts and tattoos. They were men. And you are becoming a man. And each day, your body lugs itself closer to theirs. Your father, your uncle. You are becoming.

It terrifies you. Some days.

The prospect of bills and a job and a family to lead—it's too much to fathom.

Other days, it exhilarates you, the idea of manhood—independence and strength, money and time—filling you with a sound much like wonder and awe and the beauty of making it, and suffering, too, because that is life—the questions, the questions, the unanswerable quests, those that, still half-formed, swim like gar in the deep, dark sea of your hopes for the next day and the next year and the life you fear you might eventually live.

Today, you are fixed on the idea of why Becky got him this job and how, when, why your uncle, this man with his slick rubber hands and his hammer tongue, would eventually, in time, with no regard for Becky or your grandmother or you, screw this up.

Shame pursues you. The steps of this thinking weaken, and you know better than to wish ill on another person. You know better. Your grandmother and Becky didn't raise you this way. You should only wish him the best.

But today, you can't shake it, the question of what he's done to deserve it.

Today, you stare in the mirror and inspect your teeth, and you hold an old flat razor to the soft curve of your face. The thin blade shines, lifting up its reflection to the wall and onto the ceiling, and a whole world places its weight just inside your thumb, on the palm, in the lines, like a bulb.

The water splashes in the basin.

The razor hovers near the chin.

The faucet is dull, like a piece of skin rubbed too many times.

Your feet tighten, the floor emitting its chill through the bones and the tough muscle of your soul.

So you hold the razor, and your face is not the one you held in the morning, not yours. Dark hairs have begun to jut from above your upper lip and along the full, wide jaw and chin, and your brow has grown heavier.

Behind you, your uncle's clothes puddle. Left behind, the worn clothes discarded after a shower, for someone else to pick up. A snakeskin. In the house, near where you stand. A snake has shed its skin. You kick the clothes into the corner and return to your face.

But someone is banging on the door.

And you haven't yet filled your palm with foam.

But vigorously, your uncle beats his blunt, bald fist on the small wooden door. It is a thin, flimsy door, and he might break it, you think.

A vigor like a fat cigar burning slowly is filling the house with its smoke.

"Busy," you say.

"Hurry your ass up! I got business!" He bangs again, bangs and bangs his knuckles, his talons ready to maul.

The door rattles.

Your toothbrush falls off the counter.

The water sloshes the basin.

Your toes contract into the other bones of your feet.

You drop your towel, but you can't move.

"I'm serious, Abramito! Goddamn it!"

He kicks the door, and he kicks it again, and you think it will all come tumbling down. The wall, the door, the house, your life . . .

But you don't move. And you fill your palm with foam. Slow motions. Decidedly and full of reason, you bring the foam to your face. You look in the mirror to be sure what you're doing is right. To say to yourself, You belong. And your hands go into the water.

"Fuck it!" he yells then. And he kicks the door two, three more times. The doorframe cracks. You hear it. The fissure clenches, and you step back. Walls shiver. The faucet halts its spillage and drips.

But you don't want the wall to come down, and you know it will cost money to fix whatever is broken, so you unlatch the door.

"I was talking to you," he huffs, shirtless, his chest puffing, his hair not smooth. "I gotta get ready. I'm going out."

You ignore him.

So he presses his body even closer to you, his full chest at the muddle of your own chest, so close he grazes your chin. On your neck and your mouth, his hot breath lays itself out like a towel. Against the wall, your body is stiff. In your palm, the foam shrivels, and your knees buckle in their distress.

"Put some fuckin' clothes on," he smirks, then pushes your stuff off the counter and peels off his socks.

9

"My aunt says men are dogs. Not all," Ophelia pauses, gulping.

Her hands straighten a stack of books left on the study table. Looking at you as if to say, Not you. To separate you from the pack. Not to indict you. To pull you apart from the insult she's flung like a handful of burrs.

Her eyes blink.

The library is quiet. Around you, books and more books, a stack of magazines.

"Some men," she clarifies. "Not everyone, of course, you know." Ophelia's hand crushes a ball of paper; it softly falls to your feet.

Of course.

"They mark their territory like dogs. My aunt was saying this. They stray."

She squeezes another ball of paper. The library table bends light. Your shoes squeak if you move, and so you sit very still.

I'll be different. I am different, you can't say. Let me show you.

But the words are just words, and they sit there inside you, building up, gathering weight, strengthening, wanting to taste air and be heard. Waiting for you to believe in them.

You nod. You nod, and she talks, and isn't this like most other days with Ophelia?

"I don't like my uncle," you finally say. "He's an ass," you add.

"How?" she asks.

On a folder she draws a lilac. She twirls the pencil in her hand, her face bones glistening as she listens to your attempt to make reasons. A lilac. You know it because she's told you before what's it's called, this flower, its petal clumps like clusters of sweet sugar, you know it, the lilac, because it's hers, her flower, the one she draws, the hue she loves, though you've never seen one, not in real life.

I just don't like him.

Can't trust him.

He can't control himself.

And he has a big mouth. A dirty mouth.

He always ruins shit.

This will end badly. I know.

You want to say each of these things, to serve them up on a clay platter for her to dissect with her ideas, the sharpness of her beliefs, the true things she knows about living and how to be good and what not to do, but none of it comes, not when you ask it to, not when you call it. And why is summoning so difficult? Why can't the words just jet from you, fall out, even, or spew?

The librarian announces that the library is going to close.

You glance at your phone. "He just is."

10

Write about something you want. Explain your plan to get this thing you want. Ten minutes.

The slide on the screen instructs the class to do this.

In your English class, you spend the first part of the period each day jotting down your thoughts on topics. You sit in a half-dark room, the blinds withholding daylight, and sometimes the topics connect to a story or a poem the class is reading, and the connection is overt, obvious. Other times the tie seems arbitrary, unconnected, a topic randomly selected, even.

Today, you do not care what it means. You do not wonder about the connection.

The girl beside you writes furiously, her hands wobbling as they push across the page.

Jacob stares at you, spins his pencil between his thumb and forefinger and shakes his head.

The clock on the wall speaks its little language, telling you when to start and when to stop.

Behind his desk, the teacher sits, sucking coffee through a little straw and reading a book about a father and a son and the end of the world.

You write: *I want to know about my father. My plan to obtain this is to ask. It's a simple plan. I'm just gonna ask.*

For the next nine minutes and thirteen seconds, you sit there and imagine the ask.

11

The next day you sleep until the middle of the after-noon, and you wake up with your heart in your eyes. Ter-rified, uncertain of the time of day or where you are, if the world around you is the same as you'd left it, you pop out of bed and rub your eyes as if the confusion can be wiped away. Your feet knotted, toes horning their way through sheets. Somehow, your feet lost their blood. Numb and heavy, they sink into the old mattress. Shaken, your belly crouches and splits inside itself, and the emptiness, elu-sive and forthright, is a hunger.

In the bed, you think of your question and how your uncle will respond when you pitch it. With your hands on your face, you wonder, What will he say? Will it be truth-ful? Or will he give me a box of lies? Dark fibs and behe-moth half-truths? The bed coils squawk, struggling with your weight. Your knees ache, and your toes tingle.

All the while, the world is going on without you, and the house is as still as a cemetery.

You stir, and you wish blood back to your toes, and then, at the foot of the bed, you see him. Your father. His sad, lost grin and his hands, plaster-like, full of nothing, hanging beside his thighs. A neat black suit, gray tie over a white shirt that beams crispness, shoes that shine in the dim light that slides through the curtain. But he brings a grimness, too, one of ghosts and caterpillars, hogs from pictures at school about slaughterhouses and mortal wounds and a suffering you will know only in a death that shouldn't have been.

At the foot of your bed, the figure smokes a long cigar, thick like a giant man's finger, its leaf paper brown, elephant skin, moist from his tongue. The saliva links him to the cigar as he takes it from his mouth to speak and places a hand on your sad, bloodless foot.

The lines in your foot grow hot, and at the foot of your bed, he says: "Do better. Do not end up like me, boy. Don't be nothing, nothing," he emphasizes, "like your uncle."

Your tongue is a wad of cotton. It's impossible to force a word out or whisper one or scream or cough out the silence. You gag.

"Help yourself, Abram."

At the foot of your bed, your father leans in, his mouth a poor slit from which spills the admonishment: "Do not trust the devil. Do not. Not even if he dances. Not even if he asks you to dance."

You watch the room blacken. The pecan tree scrapes against the wooden house, croaking its concerns, because a man who should have been dead manifests himself, warning you, smoking a long, fat cigar. This isn't real. Isn't real. Not real, you try to convince yourself so much that finally you say it out loud. "Not real."

To convince you, the weight of him crushes the bottom of the bed. The bed moans. The sludge in your soles quickens, sloughs off, and slowly, gradually, necessarily, you regain your footing. The veins in your feet are lines, crooked and throbbing and green, and suddenly they are able to move. And you say: "Real?"

It all makes little sense as your feet begin, slowly, earnestly, to move. So you clutch the softness of the deer blanket from Mexico to your mouth, as if a blanket or a deer might shield you as you push your body upward, against the old headboard, against the wall, away from your father.

Silly dream? There's no way . . . Your mouth full of cotton. Awful, crooked shamble of bad sleep and want? Your dead father? The father whom you never really met.

"Boy, listen to me," the man that would be your father urges. "My hour dwindles. And I have so much still to say. If you ever loved your father, boy, then do right by him. Do not follow me. So much still to tell you."

And with that, the dimness in the room is unsheathed—light bleeds in through the curtains. The headboard feels cold against your spine, and the whole room falls back into itself. As much as you wanted to find credibility in this speech from this man with the neat black suit and fat brown cigar, your throat is locked tight, impeding speech, impeding breath and thought. Sweating, you shutter yourself in the room for the remainder of the afternoon, convincing yourself none of this occurred, that you dreamed it or hallucinated it or worse, that you willed it falsely, out of loneliness or desperation, acute sadness, the kind that makes boys see things that aren't there, can't be there, not today, not ever. This happens. Perhaps it is happening to you.

And so later, when you can smell the pot of beans and the cumin from the rice, when your grandmother knocks her small hand on the door, you feign sleep.

You mumble, "No, not now—not hungry" after she says dinner is ready.

"¿Estás bien?" she asks. You okay? Then waits for your voice.

"I'll save you a plate," she mutters in Spanish tenderly, after waiting too long.

You hear her footsteps walk away. It is a soft sound, like a bird pulling its wings close to itself. And soundlessly, you look around the room, making sure he's not there, that your father, in fact, hasn't come back.

All afternoon and into the night, you lay in bed, half listening to the pecan by your window scrape its long, burdensome limbs against the roof. You listen to your heart and listen to the sewing machine making humming sounds in the other room.

Soon your uncle returns. The house walls tremble and the glass in the old windows shakes from the force with which he enters. Heavily, he steps down the hall and bangs on your door, though you hear your grandmother tell him you are sleeping, to leave you be.

When you do not stir, he enters the room, his footsteps heavy.

At the foot of your bed, he sits down near the edge and puts a hand on your ankle. He shakes it.

"Abramito, wake up."

But again you feign sleep.

"I need to talk to you. It's big, Papo. I think we got something."

But firmly, committedly, you continue faking it.

"Not right now—I gotta sleep," you slur.

He's quiet. As if contemplating.

He tries again to wake you. Shakes your leg and taps your hand repeatedly.

And again you mumble something unintelligible, turn over and give him your back.

And then he leaves, the door shutting unmistakably. Not long after that, your grandmother returns to the

room with her voice like warm tea, soothing the walls
and the difficulties of the bed and the tree that aches for
itself and scratches at the old house: "*Ven*. Come with us.
Claudio is taking me to the H-E-B. I need help getting the
turkey. Will you come?"

And for this, because it comes from her, because this
is what you do when there is love you feel for someone
you know has done ten million good things for you,
someone who has saved your life more than once and
kept you alive, you say, "Yes. Let me get up, grandmother. Just let me get dressed." The suit, the cigar, the perfect black shoes, the visit—decidedly, you agree with the
tree that you will say nothing about your father.

∾ ∾ ∾

After grocery shopping, at the table, eating *tortas* with
your family, a little girl dances with a red balloon near
the table beside you, a waitress laughs loudly, her fire
engine laugh, her earrings that shine brightly like headlights, and you ask for it straight: "Tell me about my dad."

The question from which so many other questions
are born.

It crushes the air.

Your grandmother bobbles her spoon, which falls into
her broth and splatters, and her teeth grit down.

Meanwhile, your uncle's face has gone to God.

You hold your hands in front of you, keeping them
still, allowing that stillness to not break your voice.

"My father," you say. "What was he like? I want to know."

"Abram!" your grandmother grunts. Slate faced, your
uncle shakes his head at you, pushes off the table and
gets up.

"You serious? You fucking serious?" he repeats. He knocks over his chair. The salt bottle spills white granules across the table.

The restaurant stutters and halts.

His knuckles gleam outrage and alarm, and his jaw broadens, clamps down on itself like a car that has been flattened in a junkyard. For a moment you stare at the vein that throbs in his neck, and for another, you see his eyes, which behold you with enmity and undoing.

Hold your hands, you say to yourself.

Do not look away, you force yourself.

Your grandmother has risen from her chair, her arms stretched toward your uncle, attempting to calm him down.

Near you, the little girl has stopped dancing. The waitress isn't laughing. People stare. Everyone in the restaurant stares at your family.

When your uncle exits, he leaves behind a trail of fuck yous. You watch as he yells at the darkness in the sky and starts the car. You watch as he speeds off, the engine roaring, and leaves you and your grandmother and your meal behind.

In the restaurant, there is a pall.

Except for the accordion emerging from the walls, everything is trying to restart itself.

The little girl drops her balloon string. The balloon rises. The red heart floats up toward the ceiling, its long white string like an intestine, until it tangles in a slow, spinning ceiling fan.

"Finish your food, Abram. Eat."

You watch the balloon. The little girl has stopped dancing. She watches you. Then, as if frightened or unsure, she moves toward her mother, who takes her in her arms.

∿ ∿ ∿

"How are we getting home?" you ask.

"Eat your food," your grandmother says.

She shoves her hand inside her purse, grabs for her phone. She trembles.

"Just eat," she repeats. "Eat."

So you eat. Pushing your fork around the plate, through the stale rice and the puddle of beans, across the white lettuce of the *torta*. While your grandmother busies herself punching buttons on her phone, you pretend to eat, not all of your food but enough to comply with the demand. And soon, soon enough, Becky walks through the restaurant door and comes to your table, still covered with the food-filled plates. *Conjunto* music is playing on the jukebox by the wall. There's a Spanish show featuring laughing bears on the old television suspended on a wall.

Becky sits down by your grandmother and rights the salt bottle. She picks up a napkin and sweeps the grains of salt into a neat mound and pushes your uncle's plate to the edge of the table to catch the grains while you sit and stare at your plate. The Mexican sandwich, lifeless and severe. *Tortas*, you think.

"You okay, Abram?"

You force a half smile for Becky and nod. She pats your shoulder.

You sigh and sip water, and the balloon that once was a full red heart winds tightly around the fan motor, tighter and tighter, while outside now, Becky holds your grandmother, her arms wrapping tightly around her as your grandmother weeps.

12

The past is uninhabitable.

You know this. You've been told.

In the morning, your uncle is nowhere to be found. You're fine with this, though your grandmother is worried. Worry or sadness. Perhaps both. But anger, you conclude, for sure she is angry at her one still-living son, at herself, maybe at you.

In your bedroom, you clear the nightstand and throw down a towel. You do push-ups and crunches and more push-ups and lunges, as you've done for the weeks since your uncle first took you to work out. It's a routine that suits you well. Every morning, some nights, sometimes in the middle of the day, when it feels better to smash your muscles than to sit alone with the crags that are your thoughts.

At the table, there is oatmeal and toast. Becky has left for work after spending the night, which she rarely does, and your grandmother sips her coffee.

You eat toast, and the crumbs fall on the plastic yellow tablecloth like sober reminders that not everything keeps itself intact, that things will gradually, in time, fall apart.

You tell her you only asked because you wanted to know. Doesn't everyone have the right to know where he comes from?

Meanwhile, the sun is trying to understand its loneliness.

Meanwhile, the pecan rasps its voice against the roof.

Meanwhile, the house has swollen with your grandmother's sadness.

Meanwhile, Ophelia is vibrating your phone, and you say, "Good-bye, grandmother." You kiss her forehead, and she shakes her head.

"Have a good day," she says. Solemnly. Occupied with voices you cannot hear.

Her hair is gray and not taut in her braid.

"I'm going to Ophelia's. I love you, Grandma."

The sky, however, is not gray.

Nor is it heavy. The sky is bright, full of light.

        ∾ ∾ ∾

"Go to the park with me. I made us a lunch," Ophelia tells you. You stand on her aunt's porch and marvel at her. "It feels good having the week of Thanksgiving off."

In the trees, which are bare for the season, there are birds. And there is light. Raucous chirps and cackling, flapping wings, and you wonder why there are so many of them. A flock in one tall tower of a tree.

"Hawks. They're migrating. It is almost winter," Ophelia contends.

And she's right. These birds, like people, seek someplace warmer, more comforting, less difficult to endure.

        ∾ ∾ ∾

At the mission park you sit by the river and listen to the water. You munch the tomato and cheese sandwiches she packed. The *bolillo* dough fills your mouth, and you think of saving some, a few ends of the bread, to feed to the ducks, that maybe Ophelia would like this.

"Every year they congregate down here," Ophelia says, pointing to the dark birds perched on the tree limbs.

How does she know this? you wonder.

"Do you like birds?" you ask.

"I do."

"Why do you like them?"

"Because they can fly. And because they have hollow bones."

"Hollow? I guess that's what lets them fly? Because of their bones?" you ask.

Her hand is a small egg. It rubs her cheek; the pinkish hue mixes with her almond skin. And there's Ophelia's magnificent red hair. You love it. It speaks to you of simple, tepid songs and humble operas.

She bites her sandwich and asks you midchew, "Any animal in the world . . . if you could be one, what would you be?"

Above her, the sun is furious. The sky is white. It is early in the morning, and the entire day stands before you like a field.

"Any animal?"

"Any animal."

You think. You want to say bird, because maybe that will please her, so you say, "Bird. An eagle."

"That's what you think I want to hear," she snaps. "What would you really want to be? Anything."

You know pleasing her isn't what she wants. She wants to know you, what's churning inside you like a beetle caught in a well, dipping and possibly sinking but surfacing again, fighting, striving and struggling, urgency bubbling inside of it, for sunlight, for air, for anything solid.

"Tasmanian tiger," you say, finally.

"Tasmanian tiger?"

"Sure. Why not?"

Now you are walking alongside the river. The sidewalk is cracked.

You hold her hand, because her eyes are on you, her mouth opened by breaches in words, and you hold her hand so the wide, deep crack in the ground won't trip her, so she won't fall, so nothing bad will ever befall her.

"Isn't that extinct?"

You nod. "Madagascar." You remember reading about this when you were nine.

"Humans suck. Nice one," she says. "Never would have guessed."

Her lips curl nicely, and her breath is peppermint, which reminds you of the candies you pick up that are hard white coins eddied with red, the ones your grandmother keeps in the medicine drawer.

"I'd be an iguana."

An iguana, you think. Ophelia seems nothing at all like a lizard.

Scales and long tongued, black beans for eyes, legs like broken matchsticks, but thick-skinned and robust, and so maybe, perhaps . . .

"Why?"

"There doesn't always have to be an explanation, does there?"

In front of the little waterfall by the mission, you decide not to spoil the occasion. You can be happy with this. Just a walk. Holding her warmth in your hand, listening to her stories, the new things she teaches you about birds. The park and the sound of water and the auspicious thing she just taught you about those black birds migrating and landing in San Antonio trees—it's enough.

But it's in you, you know. This want, that desire to press your mouth into hers and feel sweetness and joy and comfort and safety.

And perhaps it's inside Ophelia, too.

"We should head back," Ophelia says, finally, when you stop beneath a great oak and because perhaps she can see it in you, too, or feel it, how it bounces off your bones and through your muscles, or maybe it's coming from her, the warmth, the desire to be held and to hold and to tell and to listen—perhaps it emerges both ways.

"Sure," you agree. "We should get back," and her voice follows you, shining with dark eyes and a combustion known only by the farthest stars.

13

Quickly the week off from school goes by, and by Wednesday, Becky has stepped in and replaced the turkey left in the car when your uncle drove off, the one your grandmother will cook. As Becky and your grandmother engage in the night-before preparations, your uncle returns.

Dusk has fallen around you, yellow heaps of old light and the pinkish underbelly of the sky exposed for the trees and the leaves to witness, the sidewalk and the roofs to clutch at. You're sitting on the porch after a run when your uncle drives up.

"Get in," he tells you, pushing open the passenger door. With a hand like a pulley, he makes the door move.

Hesitantly, you approach. The music booms, and his mouth vexes you.

You don't know why exactly you get in. There's that place inside you that has always hungered for facts about your father, for an anecdote or a tidbit of a story, maybe just a thread, like he used to enjoy carnivals or his favorite food was hamburgers with refried beans smeared inside the bun from this place over on Blanco Street. You blame this. That hunger for information, anything.

"I should tell grandma."

But he smirks and says, "No worries, Papo."

He drives you to the West Side of the city. Across two freeways, over an old gray bridge that flies above train tracks and a queue of dirty boxcars. The city is lit up. Behind you, the Tower stands obediently, vigilant and formidable, above the downtown buildings, like a sentinel. Watching over you, the Tower reminds you of where you come from.

"We going to the gym?"

As the car speeds through a neighborhood with dogs running in the middle of the street and hollering children playing soccer between parked cars, your heart begins to race.

"Something like that."

When you arrive, the building appears worn. Broken bricks and grass pushing through the dented concrete. Glass has shattered and speckles the asphalt like crushed stars. With uncertainty, you exit the car, your feet heavy with hesitation, a bowling ball for a heart. You follow your uncle to a dilapidated building, the walls coming apart. You noticed a few bricks toppled over from the gym's corner edge, scattered chunks of rock. Over the door, the sign reads ALFONSO BOXING GYM.

Underneath your uncle's grip, the building's door moans and hisses. Easily, he pulls it open, but when you tug on it, the metal is heavier than any other entry you have ever gone through. The whole world inside this gym is dim. In the center of the place there is a ring, the canvas dark and stained. A single lamp bulb rains lights down from above the ring, sparse ropes of light that somehow join, somehow constitute a single beam. Arms unfurl and fling toward bags and pads, and everything appears taped up or near falling apart. It seems less than a gym, less than a place where "champs are made," as the

long, sloping banner drooping from the wall whispers.
Men grunt, and the sound of punching is everywhere.
Your neck muscles clench.

"*Compadre*," your uncle addresses someone, his hand
waving. "This here is my nephew."

A man in a little blue suit hunches over the ropes. He
spits into a bucket and turns to look at you. He wears a
dark dress shirt and a little black tie. His arms rest on the
ring's tired ropes.

Your uncle propels you forward. Pushes you with a
resolute shove that implies you know what to do, though
you don't. In fact, you don't know at all what you're supposed to be doing here, but you figure it out. Rapidly.
Glancing at the others, the bag taking a repeated beating,
the jumping rope that circles a boy's body in a steady
rhythm, the guy bent over in a dark corner, huffing and
praying and hugging his body alongside the flat sympa-
thy of the brick wall—you figure that your job is to jump
in, show what you bring.

Promptly, the man at the ropes chitchats with your
uncle and then leads you into a little office at the side of
the building, which is dust heavy and even more poorly
lit than the canvas ring. Nerves wreaking havoc inside
your heart, you follow.

Because the little office is cramped and hot, your eyes
struggle to focus, and you are sweating like every other
thing in this building is sweating. Everywhere you look
someone is hitting something—from long bags of sand to
short, bulbous ones that sprout from the ceiling and
rebound quickly, as if the bag had legs and breath of its
own and shadows. You stand beside your uncle, your
heart pounding. Certificates, old trophies, plaques adorn

the wall cracks, fat ones, tributaries that run amok and slide down the entirety of the office's walls.

"Your uncle, he tells me you fight." A thick, glum man behind the desk, his lip curling over itself. He sports a black straw hat, the ends frayed and fuzzy from age, much like his dark mustache, which also hangs over his lip.

"Yes," you say.

"I got the next Mayweather here. Let him show you what he can do," your fast-talking uncle interrupts, his quick fist on your shoulder and his gold ring gleaming.

"Fonso! Give this boy some gloves!" the old, thick man at the desk shouts to a younger guy.

Fonso rushes over with a pair of raggedy red gloves. Semirotund, the tips of the gloves look like they were once filled with air but have deflated over time. The glove skin is flaky, as if scabs once existed but have long since peeled off. Fonso tosses you the gloves.

"Find me somebody," the old, thick man says. "See what this youngster's made of."

Instantly, a boy near your age appears in the ring. He is solid, slim, too, and jets across the canvas like a fox. Perched on his muscled shoulder, a tattoo of a black eagle flexes its wide wings each time he moves. Wrapped in tape, the boy's fast fists hiss as he hits at the air, at an invisible opponent who, with each strike, is slashed in quarters and halves. Jabbing and uppercutting, his hands flaunt, float, full of what he can do to you.

So you strip off your jacket and toss it onto the floor. Sweat has gathered in your undershirt, and your teeth clamp down on themselves like locks. Your walk to the ring occupies the only two considerations in your brain—get in that ring, beat his ass.

You don't know how you'll do it.

It takes a minute for you to get your bearings.

A minute here might cost you.

Sludge overtakes your legs, and your mouth fills with mud.

Over the canvas, a naked bulb in a tin shield swings and steadies. The light it gives is dirt clad, filthy and dense, like a too-big promise.

Your uncle helps arm you with the red gloves. They add heaviness to your hands. You take a few swings. Awkward swings, off-balance and slow.

The lights everywhere else in the room are dim, and you can smell bleach.

Around you, a few of the others have halted their workouts and stare.

You climb up and through the ropes. Before entering the center of the ring, you shake your arms and stand with your chest thrust forward, full of its hopes and as broad as you can make it, as broad as the body can falsify its belief in itself. The truth is you don't know what you're doing, but you'll do it.

"What the hell y'all waiting for?" the old, thick man from the office, now standing by the tattered ropes, yells. He leans, and one of his legs wobbles. "Get the damn show on the road." With a *pañuelo*, he wipes the glow from his forehead and spits.

Your uncle grabs you by the arm and says, "Do this. Let's do this, Papo. Knock this bitch out."

When you enter the ring, a short mule of a man in a beanie hands you headgear. This is to guard your temples, but when you look at your uncle for a hint at what to do with it, how to put it on, he shakes his head firmly, says, "He don't need that shit."

So you drop the headgear over the ropes and down to the floor.

You fear the other boy is smirking, finding you inferior, a less than worthy opponent. He wears headgear, and this obscures much of his face. You shake the numbness out of your legs as you stare directly into the other guy's eyes, looking for some weakness, some hint at what he thinks of you. He's taller than you, but not by much, and after two seconds of you staring, he looks away.

Thin throated, he gulps, a swallowing you hear in your own mouth as you think of the parts of him where you'll swing. You are beefier, you know, which might benefit you in a street fight like the ones you are accustomed to, but in the ring, on this canvas, surrounded by a square of dingy ropes and men who need someone to triumph, being fast is a blessing you do not possess.

You know you have a heavier hand.

You know all it takes is one hit.

But he is faster. But he has done this before. But you don't really know what you're doing, and your hands feel as heavy as lead.

In one strike, you could put him down. One good, solid connect.

Or he could do the same to you.

It works both ways.

In the middle of the ring, your opponent holds his gloves out for you to bump your gloves with his, as you've seen fighters do on TV. There is no bell. There are no cheers. No popcorn or ring girl displaying a fancy card telling the audience some detail about the fight. No TV cameras or professional ring announcer booming his big bull voice through a fancy mic that falls from the sky.

The light is dim, and beneath your steps the canvas grumbles.

It begins, and with his first few punches, the eagle boy makes direct contact. Swift shots to the upper body, a jab to the jaw. These sting, an electricity that holds the skin in its quick grip, yet these punches do not inflict much pain, and your legs do not move swiftly. It's as if he is dancing around you, your neck twisting and following his paths, but the first couple of times you strike, he dodges, and you stumble forward, off-center, awkward, like a fool.

Later you will understand that in boxing, hits score points, and accumulating points is how you win, although in life, in the fights you are accustomed to, there is no one keeping score or taking count, no referee officiating to ensure everything is done fairly, by the rules. It's the pummeling that matters. The blood loss and the bruising and the words of exultation after the fact that matter most.

"Floating like a bee," the short, skinny man who handed you the headgear grins.

"Let's go!" your uncle shouts. "Stop pussying around!"

You do it, then. The little animal inside the box that sits in your ribs begins to stir.

In a breath, the muscles of your chest crest and shriek, and some part of you denies it will ever be owned, not by anyone else, not by you, and with this, like before, like so many times before, the lid comes off.

One blow.

It's all that it takes. From behind you, your fist grows fat like a mace, and you thrust your determined arm forward. The boy steps in, perhaps as he's been told to do, as boxers will do, you learn later, in order to absorb an opponent's power, in order to offset the coming force, and this is strange, an idea that boggles you—that to take a hit, you really do have to take it.

One pop. And you've floored him. Your fist to his mouth, and he plops down on the canvas like a useless coin, a worn shoe.

"Money, baby!! That's what's up!!" Your uncle leaps up and down and cheers, pumping his fist in the dense air, looking around at the other guys.

You jump on your opponent, straddling his belly, which is flat and limp. Blood leaks from his nose, and he's out cold. You raise your hand high in the air, but before it comes down, some guy pries you off.

The lamp above you sways. You're on your back, the canvas quaking, and two guys are tending to the fallen fighter.

He's woozy, and they're holding a rag to his face, forcing him up. Meanwhile, your uncle is cavorting, leaping out of his skin. The whole room is quiet again. Quiet and rubbing its hands together and dim.

"So, whaddaya say? When can you give us a fight? We're ready to get this shit going," your uncle trumpets, his face full of ring light and teeth.

At the edge of the canvas, you sit, and your body jerks a little, the gloves still on your fists, throbbing and hanging there by your side like two small sacks of something you cannot name. You wonder what Ophelia would think. You wonder if the eagle boy is all right.

"Well?!" your uncle says to the man who sent you into the ring. "The next Mayweather, right?"

But the man from behind the desk just smirks and says, "Come by next Monday. We can put him on one of the bags. To start . . . "

But your uncle interrupts.

With disbelief leaking from his tongue and eyes, as if he'd been the one to succumb to a punch, your uncle steps forward. "The fuck you talking about? Did we just watch the same fight? 'Cause the fight I saw, Abram knocked your guy the fuck out. What else you need to see to line him up a fight?"

From the canvas, you can see it takes the man by surprise, your uncle's approach, his insolence. It takes the man a few seconds to compose himself, and when he responds, he straightens out his tie and breathes in air, dropping his shoulders and holding his chin firm. He says, "First, the kid has to learn to box. He's too big now. So he needs to lean up. You can come back on Monday. We can start him off on a bag."

And to this, your uncle bites his jaw and shakes his head, and you're afraid of what comes next. But the stout man never takes his eyes off your uncle, and everyone else around you is watching and stepping in a few steps closer, too. A few of the fighters have amassed behind the gym owner, and your uncle has nowhere to go but out. Angrily, he storms out, flinging the heavy door open. You aren't fast enough to follow him without staring at the gym owner ruefully and shrugging your shoulders, then grabbing your jacket and running as fast as you can to catch up to your uncle, who is already backing up the car.

14

"You know, I'm going to stop fighting. No more. But this is the deal," you tell Ophelia beneath the pecan tree in front of your grandmother's house. She's come by to drop off cookies she baked for you and your grandmother and Becky—chocolate chip with pecans harvested from the tall tree underneath which you stand.

"No more?" Ophelia's eyes light themselves up, as if a tiny machine inside of them suddenly, fondly and fiercely, has summoned up courage.

You wield the cookies, still warm, and their heat bleeds through the plate into your fingers.

The day looms. Raking leaves, Thanksgiving dinner and football on TV for you—for Ophelia, it's helping her aunt cook, then going to her other aunt's house for dinner and then cleaning up. There are things to do, so many things. But often in life there are necessary minutes, minutes that cannot be spared or postponed or squandered. These are moments to be had before the routine of the day starts, before anything else happens.

"Really? You promise?" Ophelia asks.

Her eyes stare into you the way someone can show you how much of her is there with you, not with her worries about chores or with her friends or with her homework, but there, with you, listening to you, thinking of each word you say and how it means something precious and precise to her. Her eyes ask you to give her some part of a promise.

Later in life, you learn that in these small moments she was teaching you how to love—if only you'd listened.

"My uncle took me to a gym. I'm going to be training. In a gym. I could be the next Mayweather. Can you imagine it?"

Ophelia's smile is as big as the river. Her heart shines through her eyes, and her laugh is the kind that always makes you think of goodness.

"Like boxing? A pro?"

You nod. "Everything is gonna change."

She smiles, and you hold her hand, and she asks you if you'll text her throughout the day.

"I have work to do, and my mom might be Skyping. Thanksgiving, you know." Her cheeks as red as the new gloves your uncle promised to buy for you to wear when you train.

"Of course. Of course."

You hope her mother comes through. You hope a bad thing has not happened. Inside, you wish you might do something to ensure this, to help fulfill the promise her mother made her to come back. By this time, you don't know what it is, this little fire in your gut, how it rises up in the darkness like little stars shining in the night sky over the buildings and the houses, over the river that cuts through the city and the short, squat trees with their leaves falling to the earth to finish their lives. Maybe this is Love? Maybe this is the feeling people spend their entire lives pursuing, this thing people have suffered for and given their lives to have and to guard and to seek?

Across the street, a man removes lights from two large cardboard boxes. He lays the strings of lights along the ground, then stops his work to watch you and Ophelia. From their porch, his wife staggers three electric white deer who'll roam their yard until Christmas. You eat a cookie and wave to the couple while holding the plate of cookies in one hand. Ophelia waves, too. He smiles, and so does his wife, and you offer them a cookie. Politely, he shakes his head, and she mouths the words "No, thank you." Together they go back to laying out the lights and preparing the white deer. The man starts nailing the strings onto the house.

For a minute, watching Ophelia walk down the sidewalk, you imagine yourself like this man. It is a nice thought, pleasant, and it holds in its warmth Ophelia and joy and every happiness you can fathom, and for the rest of your life, it is the only thing you can ever believe you want.

15

All afternoon you think of the next time you will go to the gym. Weights or boxing, you don't care. The anticipation fumes in your hands, hot like a coal.

Your Uncle Claudio has disappeared. Your Uncle Claudio with his fast car and his tough talking, his fancy clothes and his gold and the girls who all like him—you never thought he'd do something good, but he has.

In the kitchen, your grandmother and Becky work on the turkey and manage the sides, and from time to time you hear their laughter, warm and buttery and brimming with calm.

"*Ya mero.*" Almost done, your grandmother tells you, leaning over the sofa's thin back and kissing your hair.

good cookies. dang good. You text Ophelia that you've eaten five, maybe six.

:), she replies.

wanna go to riverwalk? lots of lights.

tomorrow?

tonight.

tomorrow. yes. can't tonight.

It is the best day in the world, and you eat two more cookies, but your grandmother slaps your hand. "You'll ruin your appetite," she says in her sweet Spanish.

"*Ay*, let him," Becky interjects. "He's young. Not like us," she jokes. "He can always work it off in the gym."

She smiles, and you smile, and your grandmother pouts playfully, dropping her face into Becky's shoulder so that Becky can wrap her arms around her and make it all right.

Smoldering is the word to describe how you want to go back to train. You sit in front of the TV, and you go to your room to do push-ups, counting them out by twenty-fives, then add crunches, and you think that if you get some money, you'll buy some dumbbells, 20s or 30s, maybe 25s. You do this a few times, until your arms ache and your belly is on the verge of a cramp.

"This is the big time, kiddo," your uncle on the drive home gripped your knee and told you. His teeth were shiny, white like spearmint gum squares, his arms muscled like knots in the ropes the coaches make you pull in PE. "If that weak-ass gym don't believe in you, I can. Learn to box? Calling you too fat? What the hell! Like we wasn't watching the same beatdown. We got this," he added. "Big time. All you, Papo. Our lives are gonna change."

Each time he picked something up or when he showed you his moves, all jabs and uppercuts, you thought perhaps your arms would grow as rippled and large as your uncle's. Who'd have thought you'd ever want to believe yourself anything like him? In the back-yard Uncle Claudio has promised to hoist a punching bag for you to hit while you're at home. You can see yourself going at this bag, unleashing on it, beast mode. To this, you smirk. *Beast mode.* You can see Ophelia cheering you on, and you imagine all the stuff you can buy her and how you'll pay off your grandma's bills and get her a car and thank Becky for all the good things she'd done for you over the years.

When it's time to eat, Becky says grace. It is a nice prayer, and you know one day this will be your job, to say grace. Your plate is as full as can be. You've eaten nearly half your meal when the doorknob squeaks and you hear the jangle of keys.

"Where have you been?" your grandmother asks when your uncle shows up with a bag of potatoes and a pie.

"Around." His chin dribbles with scruff, and his eyes droop as if they haven't shut themselves and the daylight has been too bright. He drops the bag of potatoes near the sofa and suckles air far back into his lungs.

Before you'd never seen your uncle for more than a few hours. But now that he is back in your grandmother's house, you've convinced yourself that maybe, just maybe, he isn't that bad, that although he's not perfect, there is enough good in him.

"Well, sit. Join us, *m'ijo*. Let me get you a plate."

Something like happiness coats your grandmother's voice, and you wonder if it is coating or perhaps the happiness is more deeply ingrained than just this artifice, so momentary and fleeting.

But your uncle is silent.

Your heart beats very fast, and you bite your lip and stare over at Becky, whose face has turned to stone.

"Let me serve you. Here, *¿qué quieres?*" What do you want? your grandma asks him.

"*Nada*, Amá." Nothing. His mouth lags and the words emerge slurred, as if they've been thrown against a wall and are compelled by gravity to slide downward. "I can't stay that long. I have some stuff to handle."

Your grandmother's face drops. And she drops the plate she was about to fix him, her anxious fingers fumbling to forgive themselves. When she speaks, the sound that emerges is a low, even tone: "Well, perhaps just some pie. Perhaps maybe just some pie, no? Maybe a *tamal*? They're very good. Can I get you that?"

Watching this, hearing it, you remind yourself of why he shouldn't have come.

Leave. Leave now. Get out! you imagine yourself shouting, and then the voice inside roars like a big rig barreling down the highway. Rightfully, you would pummel the man who'd hurt your grandmother again and did whatever he did or didn't do—who knew—to or for your father.

"Just let him go," you say. "Just go," you tell him. "You can't even stay for Thanksgiving?! Man, she doesn't ask you for shit."

"Abram!"

"No, Ma. Let him. Let him," he scoffs. "He wants to man up and talk down, let him. He wants to step up like a man. You drop one little boy in a bunk-ass boxing ring, and you think you're a badass now?"

Your uncle is talking to you now. He's up in your face, and his breath is hot like an iron, wrong blooded, indignant. And you know this feeling, having another man in your face, provoking you, trying to push you down. It is familiar and different at the very same time, and your uncle is present, and the world is very old, so perhaps this is a battle that has compressed men and made them for eons. Chiseled them and placed fire inside of their mouths.

You don't know what to say or what to do that is good. You want, you want to knock the shit out of him. But Becky places her hand firmly on your leg, and she squeezes you, pushing every ounce of restraint she can muster into your muscles and bones.

"Abram." She says it firmly. Becky's voice bolsters and strikes at the inside part of you that is ready to strike out. "Abram," she repeats more firmly.

But you push back from the table, and your chair, the one beneath you, reaches for another part of the floor, one that can hold it and you and maybe fix the slenderness that has whittled itself between you and the control you wield over the overcrowded fuss happening in your veins, a fuss that riles the little animal in the long cage of your ribs.

"I'm not afraid. Not afraid of you. You're gonna leave anyway."

"Abram," your grandmother urges. "Leave. You go to the room. Abram! Abram!" But your fist has a fury inside it.

But the little animal inside you bares its teeth and is ready to attack.

You smirk, and your chest expands. The vein in your neck grows thick, and it thuds. It is a line full of blood that says its name loudly against the hull of your skin.

So your uncle's chest holds right up to yours. You can feel his breath on your face like a lantern, because his teeth can do little more than hold back his air. He pushes forward with his chest and tries to topple you.

You meet his challenge: "Big man! Why don't you get in your car and go somewhere. Go and drive off and don't look back."

"Abram!! *¡Basta!*" your grandmother screams, squeezing her frail body between the two of you while Becky tries to hold her back.

"The two of you, stop!!" Becky yells.

His eyes cannot bore holes into you, though they try.

"Man, enough of this shit! *¡Basta!*" your uncle yells.

Your grandmother pushes you back. The line in your neck, full of blood, quakes beneath her hands. Your spine feels the wall. "Go, Abram! Go to your room!"

"Damn!!!" he yells.

But your heart is snagged, its whole husk hardening and full of blood. By then, you're halfway to the hall and stop only to turn back and listen to the front door slam shut. The car roar is a false triumph, the wheels squealing as they imprint black scars on the cold asphalt.

16

major drama. shit., you text Ophelia, but she doesn't reply.

You figure she's busy. So you do so many push-ups your arms crumble, the bones bleed out of their rhythms and marrow. What's left is a pile of ache in the middle of the bedroom floor.

∾ ∾ ∾

By the time Ophelia responds, Becky has let herself into your room and given you a speech you will never dislodge from the fibers that make up your heart and your bones and every dream you felt growing inside you about how to live your life as a man, not any plain or unmotivated man, but a good man. And that's how she starts. And you listen because the words she gives you are very much like the little light of stars.

"I am proud of you. Funny, no? To hear me say that after all that. But I am, Abraham. I am proud of you. Before I came in here, I thought about what to tell you. I didn't ask your grandmother for permission. Because you and I both know how she thinks. But I sat at the table and thought for myself. Like if I should tell you anything at all or if I should demand that you go back and finish eating, like if nothing had happened, just pretend everything was all right. But we both know that's not right. Pretending shit isn't happening, it's the worst thing we can do. Too much of that happens around here. But it doesn't have to be that way.

"So how does it have to be? The truth is, there are enough bad men in the world, Abraham. Bad women, too. People who thieve and lie and hurt others. They only care about themselves, about what they can get regardless of how it turns out for others. You have to be a good man. I'm telling you. There is enough bad in the world. You can see it on the news every day. Or every night. I can tell you stories. People getting hurt all over the place, killed and raped and shot and stolen from. I'm telling you today, from this moment on, you must be one of the good guys, Abraham. You must. You must. You must. You're a smart guy, a strong guy, and you have to do good with what you have. Anything else is a waste. Anything else means all the sacrifices your grandmother has made, every sacrifice I have made in helping her help you, then it was for nothing, because we believe in you and that's only worth a damn if you believe in yourself, *m'ijo*."

You sit for a long while and listen. It's the words that she's giving you, how they disperse themselves in the room, over the bed that once belonged to your father, across the floorboards and the blue pillowcases, through the gray plastic blades of the old fan, only to coalesce again inside of you, where they're meant to land all along. And so that's what you do, as you listen, you breathe—and you open yourself to permit her voice to enter you, to merge and emerge and reconfigure the parts of you that have felt lost and haven't made sense until now.

When she's done, when her syllables have reassembled themselves in the new parts of the you they've made, then you hold that last word in your heart, and you fall into her body, quivering, slobbering a handful of hard, brave sobs, spittle spewing from your limp mouth as you huff and break apart from the inside in order to be made whole again.

That night, you sit with Becky on the cold wood of your floor, and she grips you tightly, her arms bolder than any stone God has ever made, firmer and more loving than anything you might ever have projected coming from your father, who is no longer among the living, and your mother, who left. Over you, the light in the room is dim, and the bed winces each time Becky's back shifts against the side of the old mattress and box spring. Above the roof, the sky is black, and there are stars offering the world the certainty of their light, and the pecan tree, wanting to make itself known, wanting to give voice to its wants, scrapes against roof each time there is a breeze.

At the table again, after your grandmother joined the two of you on the floor, after her hot tears and her shaky voice apologized to you for pushing you away, the three of you sit and listen to the old country music Becky loves, a Christmas album. Together, you cut the Bill Miller pecan pie, the kind Becky loves, and your grandmother makes coffee, and like this, pouring sugar and eating pie, listening to Reba McEntire and watching the steam from the turquoise mugs form marvelous white swans, you remember why this all started.

"I don't think he should come back," you say, chewing pie and crust. "I don't think you should let him back."

Without pause, your grandmother reaches for your hand and holds it like a button that gathers a loose shirt.

She gently pulls your fork from your grip and places it on your plate, and she looks you in the eyes and nods. "I know. I know."

This is how you tell Ophelia the story.

It's a briefer version you impart, though, because the two of you, the next night, sit underneath the stars, floating along in a river barge that drifts beneath a million lit cypress trees that line the River Walk's banks. The air is cold, and Ophelia nuzzles beside you, her sweater the color of turnips and her red hair as red as a heart. You hold her hands in your coat, which you've wrapped around her, and each time she speaks, her breath dances its soft movements in tough puffs of white feathers, the puffy fur of some fantastic bird. The sky is dark and alive with brightness: blues and bold tangerines, greens and enduring reds, chili-pepper yellows, pebbles of light or buds of small fires, constellations too near the heat of your bodies to have any name other than joyousness, than calm, than wonder. The more you stare at the lights clinging to the cypress trees, hanging over the river, you see a galaxy of ideas: ten years from that day, a watermelon cracking open at a children's birthday party, and kayaking down a fast-skinned river with Ophelia, and the whole white moon over your trees over a bonfire where you sit and hold Ophelia as she plays a guitar, all of it, alabaster white, and your house, your house filled with laughter and swans and barbecue, a baby sitting in the middle of the yard while you tell stories about when you and Ophelia were young, a watermelon, a tree, a baby, the moon and a river . . .

"I love the fact that you wait," Ophelia whispers into your neck. "Sometimes I worry that you won't like me because of it. That someone might steal you away," she tells you with a fissure in the full flesh of her voice. "But if that was the case, then, like my mother said, a man who can't wait for you isn't meant to be yours. And it's true."

You smile. You don't need any words. You hold her hand and squeeze it a bit, and those are your words. That is enough.

"I want us to be good people," she says. And the stars fall then, because you hold Ophelia to your chest, and she holds you back, and you laugh, the two of you swaddled in river light.

17

Fathom.

Tell me, what is it you plan to do with your one wild and precious life?

The little handwritten card on the counselor's desk asks this and tells you Mary Oliver wrote it, the bold black letters direct and singular, nodding to you and your thoughts, which whorl, much as they do any day. And you read it—*your one wild and precious life*—study its sounds, its shadow, saying every word to yourself, under the heaviness of your tongue, with patience and vigor and lust for someplace you have never heard of before but know in your bones is there, possibly, somewhere in the near vicinity of your not-far-off future. What will you do with it? you ask yourself. Your life. Waiting. The clock ticking. You know you want Ophelia to be part of it, somehow. The clock on the wall shaking its little hand like a long, slow-moving queue of ants. The counselor with her back turned to you, the phone cocked between her ear and shoulder, jotting notes hurriedly in a small black notebook, her voice pleasant and matter-of-fact and solid.

When she comes to you, she asks simply, "How are you, Abraham?"

"Well."

"'Well'? I like that. Not everyone knows to use 'well' when asked how he's doing."

You wait.

"It's a compliment. I'm giving you a compliment," she says.

Her hair is pulled back behind her ears, and its ends hang from her shoulders like the soft yellow grasses of a field you once saw in a book.

The phone rings.

It rings again, a few more times, and the counselor glances at the number, as if deciding to answer it or not, then checks her watch, punches one button on the phone and proceeds.

"I'll just cut to the chase. I'm changing your schedule. You can't be in the same classroom as a student with whom you've fought. So we are changing your schedule."

"Okay," you say. "Okay."

She hands you the white sheet, the class list neat and ordered and perfectly black.

Again you stare at the card on the counselor's desk about preciousness and wildness and life.

"You have one more year, Abraham," she says.

One more year, you think, walking slowly back into the hallway.

∾ ∾ ∾

That afternoon, you put your face to the pillow. Inside, the pillow of your heart inflates and exhales, exhales and inflates. On some nights, when the street is as silent as a shoe, the heart is a pillowcase, just a pillowcase, filling slowly with air. You could live this way: slowly filling, emptiness overcome with weight. You think of Ophelia sitting at her desk, her face pressed into a book. Or at her computer screen, waiting to hear her mother's song. Or on her bed, with her hands in her letters or thinking about you. Each thought simple and necessary and comforting.

But tonight, tonight, the world is small, and the moon is heavy, hovering with loneliness or something like that, the loneliness of a satellite or the lone unpicked fruit left on the vine. For an hour, you lay there, your eyes paying attention to the light. The moon with her suffering, her oddly, less fully formed skull splotched with scars and eyeless. The tree scratching the roof.

sup., you text Ophelia.

Someone told you once there was a rabbit on the moon. And a little boy. What, a life? What do they do?

Your grandmother once told you the moon falls apart from all the bad things that have happened to her but is so strong that she puts herself together again and again and again. Every night, each month. For eternity.

Sometimes you believe your father is like this, capable of being put together somehow, stitched or glued or composed as one would piece together a broken plate, a small statue whose arms have dislodged from the torso.

homework :/
tell me a poem i should read
will look for one
big moon outside
i heart the moon
me, too
, too = smart :)
new English class
yay
sweet dreams
dont forget freewrite homework
ok

∾ ∾ ∾

In the morning, you wake with your two hands in fists. From the crouch in which you've slept, your back aches, but light fills the room, and your eyes open themselves. Your uncle is not home and hasn't come back since Thanksgiving. Your grandmother is already off to work. The house is yours.

You sit at the table with the tacos your grandmother left and empty pages in the new journal from the new class.

These moments alone with yourself: both the best of times and the worst. No words can expound upon the joy of solitude, how picking what to watch on TV, how not being told to make your bed or to take out the trash, how the silence, that silence, is essential and listless and genuine. No syllables can defy the loneliness, though. How it creeps, how it sneaks, how it waits. In the part of your heart where you think of your father, where your mother sits on a couch and paints her toenails or drinks a cold beer or laughs rambunctiously, all giggles and lipstick and long conversations with a homegirl, there, in that part, you feel it. For a few hours, the world belongs to you—it is silent, and you are fine with this. Silence and tacos and a little bit of thinking. Makes for a good journal. Makes a good start to a screwed-up day.

18

The night your uncle returns, the Spurs are on TV, and your grandmother sits with joyousness on her body like a shawl. It is a quiet joy. Like a small blackbird's, one that has found some simple morsel it enjoys and, for that briefest of moments, to live for.

When you are dead, you will remember her. Like this. Joyous. Wrapped in her happiness. Enthralled by the smallness that ignites us, each of us, having that one or two or maybe, if we're lucky, three or five things that bring us there. Your grandmother and her beloved Spurs. The clenching of her eyelids in those perfect moments when tension escapes the court and a free throw matters more than a kiss, her jaw that also tightens in those delicate, teetering exchanges. The prayers, tenderness whispered for a single basket or one measly point, but points that she yearns for, hankers after, fundamental scoring—silly, really, she'll confess later through her small laughter, an exhaling that animates her chest and signals relief once the game has been clinched.

Tonight the Spurs are winning. Easily. Duncan and Ginóbili and Parker light up the screen. Danny Green and Kawhi Leonard. And this brightens your grandmother.

"You think this year they'll go all the way, Grandma?" you ask her. This excites her. The promise of it.

"Con el favor de Dios." If God wills it, she says.

"Something to drink?" she offers from the kitchen as the game goes to commercial.

Before you can respond, before you can begin to ask yourself about thirst, the door begins to budge, and it is your uncle, flat-footed, the darkness behind him. The door wobbles before it lets him in, and it slaps the wall, and your uncle stands there, staring at you, holding a red-nosed pup.

Blankness swamps his eyes. His mouth askew, he holds a dark red thing in his arms, a creature too busy squirming, its paws vying for freedom, to whimper or whine.

"I bought her for you, Abraham. I thought you might like a dog. A boy should have a dog," he says and shuts the door with his foot.

From the kitchen, your grandmother gasps. She holds her hands in a knot in front of her legs. And her face quakes.

When your uncle releases the red thing in his arms, the pup darts about the floor rambunctiously and wags her tail and nearly knocks over a lamp, bites at your toes through your socks and scampers away, playfully smashing her snout full against the wall.

When she darts for the Christmas tree, you reach for her, and her belly is fat, as if a grapefruit resides beneath the soft pink flesh.

"She's part pit bull. Her name is Destiny," your uncle tells you as he rummages through the refrigerator. The fridge light on his face reveals torpor, a weariness you haven't witnessed in him before.

From the counter, your grandmother watches. Motionless, she holds her hands in a bind in front of her lap.

"But you can change it." He stuffs a handful of chicken into his mouth and chews. "Her name, if you don't like it."

"She's mine?"

"If you want her."

He decides on a beer, cracks it open without thinking.

Lucy, you think. I'm gonna name her Lucy. Or maybe Diamond or Baby Girl. But you don't know, you aren't sure.

The final buzzer: the commentators start on the Spurs and their win.

"Grandma, can I . . . " But when you turn to complete the question, she is already gone.

For the next hour, while your uncle thumbs through his phone at the table, you sit on the floor, playing with Destiny, whom your uncle has given you. Soon you fall asleep with the dog in your bed, her wet nose nuzzled into your chest, her snoring even and soothing, a white noise swamping the tree that scratches the roof and the whizzing of cars crushing their dark tires into the road.

In the morning when you wake, your grandmother hasn't made breakfast. The house is quiet.

You grandmother's disapproval stings you.

Because the sun fills the sky, you take a rope from the storeroom and tie the little dog named Destiny to the tree. Out of leftover boards from the old fence, which you helped Becky mend when you were in eighth grade, after half the fence had fallen from a windstorm that knocked down a whole pecan limb, out of these parts and pieces you fashion a little house for the dog. Destiny watches while you build it, the makeshift shelter where she'll spend her days, you intend, while you're at school or unable to keep vigil. It's a sad little doghouse, splintered and uneven, and you worry over its inadequacy, so you wrap a blue tarp like a scarf around the dwelling, hoping it will shun rain, deter hard winds. You figured you might sneak her in at night or something.

"Abram, I have changed my mind." Your grandmother stands at the door to the back porch, behind you, her words carving a small half smile on the bottom half of her face.

"What do mean?" You pause your work.

"I have changed my mind about the dog."

"Really?" In the mud you drop the hammer and spit the nail you've held in between your teeth. The metal leaves a taste in your mouth that reminds you of nickels.

"Yes. Yes. I know how bad you've wanted a dog, and for a long time I have said no, mostly because I don't want to have to clean up after an animal inside the house, but it's getting cold now, and I suppose we could keep her in the little laundry room."

The blue tarp flaps in a gust of wind. The little dog whines and cocks her head sideways, in a tilt, eyeing you fully.

"Can she sleep with me at night?"

"I don't see why not. But if she makes a mess, you have to clean it. You have to because I'm not cleaning up dog *caca*."

You smile big. You can agree to this.

Quickly, you jump on the porch and fly to your grandmother, who stands at the doorway to the little laundry room at the rear of the house. The laundry has piled up, but she holds you and forgets about anything else. Immediately, the dog jumps to her feet and runs to you, squealing. But the rope hinders Destiny.

For the next hour, you keep her with you in the little room at the back of the house. With an old gray towel, you wipe her red fur, and you pick the fleas off her coat, and she licks you and rubs her wet nose against your chest and arms, and you hold her like a baby, so that she falls asleep with her legs tucked into themselves and drools and snores and whimpers from some wonderful dream, whose events you will never know, that is zooming its course inside her little brain. You hold her, and you hear her heartbeat, and you promise, I will never leave you.

19

When you tell Ophelia about the pup in your life, she's all ears. The next day at school she sits with you at lunch, and this causes the whole table of your school friends, the place where you usually sit, to stare.

"Look at this," a boy with a muzzle for a mouth says. Large, oversized teeth, a baseball cap pulled backward. He points.

You and Ophelia sit at your own table, an empty spot by a tall window at the end of the long table occupied by the special education kids and their aides.

"She's with him?" a girl with a flower for a mouth says loud enough for you to hear.

The spot inside you that grows hot, that spoiled spot where the little animal sometimes lives and leaps from, that spot stirs and says its name and menaces, but you do not jump, and you do not react, you don't say a thing to the muzzle-mouthed boy or the girl with the flower for a mouth, and you hold steady, and you stare at Ophelia's hands, at her simple wrists and her perfect little hairs, the modest gold ring her mother gave her, which she never takes off, her fingernails, which are unpinned and natural and not painted. They tap on the table easily, her fingernails making a little melody that emanates from their bodies, the light from the sky entering the window and gleaming off her skin that your grandmother describes like warm coffee.

The girls who are her homegirls stare, too. Nice girls, the smartest girls in school. Always neat and well groomed, with their straight A's and their good teeth. Girls who might not ever give you or your few friends the time of day but who'd never be ugly. Two tables away, their eyes tell a story of worry. The trepidation takes the form of whispers and quick glances, disapproval and head shaking, coupled with the pretense that none of them are judging.

On the other hand, your friends grow excited and mouthy. But they know better than to say shit. They sit with their trays and stuff their jaws and laugh loudly, louder than is necessary, and you know something is different, though you can't say what it is.

You wonder if her aunt still doesn't like you.

You remembered to pull out her chair and to ask her about her day.

"Revising my last few college essays," she tells you. "You'll be doing this next year," she adds and sips water from a green bottle. You grab the bottle's cap as it rolls away.

You smile, and it feels like your mouth is splaying your face, pulling it back and forth and turned toward your ears, making it so that if you're not careful, everything might come out. You remember to ask if she wants anything else after she's eaten most of the cherry tomatoes and the sandwich her aunt sends with her from home. "We should be eating more fruits and greens," she urges you, chomping a red glory and holding the plastic bag open for you to pick from.

And you actually consider it. Eating more veggies. So
you grab a red orb and pop it into your mouth, and chewing the sweetness procures a brief glimpse of your life
one day, a future where the two of you at the grocery
store go aisle through aisle, your basket vibrant and leaf
filled, her voice instilling the store with sweetness.

As you're eating, she says she wants to go the library
when you're done, and you set aside your plan to mess
around outside with your friends and a football, and you
say, "Yeah. Sounds good."

Before you know it, she's chuckling with the librarian
and helping you pick out a book.

It's a book about zombies.

"Why zombies?" you ask.

"Why not?" the librarian, a pretty woman with dark
hair to her shoulders and a laugh full of sparks, says back.

"Something else, maybe?" Ophelia suggests.

Ms. P, the librarian, asks about things you are into,
and Ophelia recommends a book about dogs. She and
Ophelia apparently are friends.

"He just got a new dog. A puppy," Ophelia tells her.

"Aww. I love dogs. I have two myself. What did you
name her?" the librarian asks, leaning in a bit to listen to
your voice.

"Destiny," you tell her, with your hands behind your
back, with your voice low and detouring, because you
can't think of what you'll change it to.

You've been at this school three years, and it's hard to
believe this is the first time you've ever checked out a
book.

"Never too late," Ms. P chimes. "My neighbor is eighty-
six years old, and he just learned to read. He had to leave
school when he was young so that he could help work the

fields. It was what people did in those days. Now you can't pry a book or the newspaper out of his hands." She laughs kindly. "For Christmas I think I'm getting him a Kindle." And smirks. Her eyes are bright. Her blouse is blue, like the color of the pen Ophelia uses to write in her notebook.

"That's sweet." Ophelia is touched. "Imagine that," she'll tell you as the bell rings and you're off to your classes, "being eighty years old and barely learning to read. It's awesome."

You like this about her, how she's gentle and gets happy over the simplest things, how she can see the magic in other people's lives, in the things others would easily overlook. You want this. Think it significant and precious and wonder why there's not more of it in the world. You want this part of her to be part of your life, and you would to do anything to protect that tenderness so that it always, forever, has a safe place to live. And yet, because or perhaps in spite of this, there is a part of you, too, that questions whether you are good for her, if she's not out of your league or placing her kindness at risk by being so close to a guy like you.

On the way home you run as fast as you can, through the alleys and across the side roads, which no one drives unless they're getting off work and heading off to a shift at some odd hour of the day or engaged in wrongdoing. Above you, the power lines heat themselves, their voices quipping and aware in the cold December air. The sky is yellowing, and the trees send their branches like hard chutes, dark trajectories, into the dimming light.

When you walk into your house, your grandmother sits at the kitchen table watching her shows, and she smiles big, glad that you made it home safely. In the laundry room, Destiny has spent the better part of the day gnawing on a soup bone your grandmother gave her, but quickly, upon hearing your voice, she drops the bone and paws at the door for you.

"Welcome home, schoolboy," your uncle says with a smirk.

He grins like a very muscular grinch, you think. At the sofa, his feet propped up on the little coffee table, he thumbs the remote control, replaying a sports show where an MMA fighter roundhouses a lesser opponent. The vanquished falls flat on his back, and the Octagon erupts. Your uncle leans in, and his face becomes the color of the screen.

"You see that!" he yells. Electricity propels his eyes.

From the kitchen your grandmother shuts her eyes. There is a word search in front of her, the lanyard that holds her reading glasses dangling from her neck like a headache that's threatening to take hold. You let the little dog in and sit by your grandmother, holding the dog as she bites at your chin and nibbles at your thumbs.

That night you will thumb through the book about dogs, then you will lay in bed for an eternity. Destiny will curl at your feet and sleep. You will replay the events of the recent weeks, from the weight work at the gym to the second it took for you to lay out the guy in the ring and the drama with your uncle at Thanksgiving and the look on Ophelia's face when she brought over her schoolbag before lunch and said, "May I sit with you?"

You always want to remember that look. Her eyes like two lifetimes, two whole lives, that bright and splendid— it is the sweetest look in the world. Maybe this is how mothers look at their babies when they first see them. Maybe not. Maybe it is a baby's first glimpse of light or of the whole forest or of the sea. Maybe it's the moon making herself whole, feeling accomplished and joyful and ready. You scribble some of this down in your journal, jotting ideas about love and what you will do with yourself, with your one wild, precious life.

The world is wonderful, and you think maybe you might love Ophelia, if that is the word for it . . .

But you think of the roundhouse kick, too, wondering how challenging it would be to do that, to learn it, to summon it up during a clash. How much force you'd have to muster from the hip joint and through the long fibers of the leg and the foot. You think of the other guy's chin, how in slow motion the face loses its place in the world, how it smears like a can of paint thrown against a floor or a wall, how it becomes less than a face, more like a contortion of putty or a cartoon.

But you don't stay on the roundhouse for long.

You think Ophelia's is the look of happiness and that every man should have someone to give him this look. And every woman, too. Every child. Everyone. It's the look that says, I'm glad to see you. I'm glad I know you. I like you. I'm glad you're here.

Who wouldn't want to hear those things? Or feel them?

Who wouldn't want to live immersed in happiness and kind ways?

Beside you, Destiny snores, and she twitches, her nose jerking slightly, so you pull her closer to you, snuggle her to your belly and breathe. You like the idea of Destiny, of holding her near your body and listening to the hour your heartbeat meets hers.

You think, though, perhaps I should change her name.

The bed creaks.
What would you name her?
You put off sleep as long as you can.

～ ～ ～

Ordinarily, when you think of your uncle, you remember his eyes. Because your uncle has very brown eyes, and his voice is sometimes made of rusted tin or iron, and other times it is heavier, like steel or another hard metal encased in mud. It's the kind of voice that coils or booms when it has to.

But when he enters your room, your uncle's voice is a pilot light. So blue. Easy to ignite but calm and steady, floating, full of heat.

"Abraham. Wake up. I need you to hear me," he mutters and shakes you from your sleep.

Your Destiny doesn't budge, but you open your eyes and see your uncle, his silhouette, sitting at the far edge of your bed, near your ankles and feet.

"I got it. I got a way for us to win big."

"Oh. I wanna go back to sleep. Can you tell me this in the morning?" you slur, burying your face in a pillow.

"I can get you a fight. Cash, Papo. Just give me the green light. Tell me you're down."

"When?"

"Just give me your word," he tells you. "Your word. A real man gives his word."

You hesitate. There's that part of you that makes itself known when something's not right, makes itself loud and apparent and full of itself, which is necessary and urging you to trust it. But sometimes you don't. Sometimes you neglect it, that little noise that presents itself from the gut. Sometimes you turn down its volume or turn up some other volume so that you don't have to hear out the part of you that warns, that protects, that won't just go along. And sometimes you just tell it to shut up.

"Do this for me. It's Christmas, Papo. We need a good Christmas here," he pleads. "Say you'll do this."

So you do. You shut off the inkling inside of yourself that asserts this isn't good. Your heart in a knot, you agree. You tell him you'll do it. You don't really know why, but you give in, and you give him your word.

20

It happens on a Thursday.

The evening has come, knocking its rose claws against the horizon.

Your grandmother stands at the pecan tree with a bedsheet, which disperses itself onto the grass, a perfect soft square. She stares. Ophelia stands beside her, holding a bucket, wearing your black-gray hoodie for warmth. The bedsheet is white and becomes a square. The tree bark is tough looking, rough to the eye, and the tree is very tall.

"Are you sure, Abramito?" your grandmother asks.

"Be careful," Ophelia begs.

From the front door, Destiny bangs her paws against the glass and whines. Your grandmother hushes her to no avail.

Full of its unapologetic limbs, the tree towers above the house. Thick, grim appendages stretch across the radiance that is the sky, over the house and over the road, and from these limbs, thinner, slimmer, weak-looking limbs tremble in the breeze. The sun is fierce. The tree appears lit, a silhouette of hot paint.

When you climb, you place each hand in front of the next methodically, decidedly, unafraid to err but precisely aiming for the fullest, steadiest parts. Some branches you avoid, because they tremble too much before your eyes.

"*Ay*, be careful!" your grandmother yells, the corners of her mouth wrinkled like a tussle of tissue. She pulls her hands from the pockets of Becky's Carhartt, and they cover her mouth.

"It's okay."

"He climbed like this before. One time. When he was in seventh grade," she tells Ophelia. "He lost his key and instead of calling me, because I was at work, he climbed the tree to get in the house through the window at the top."

It's true. You climbed this tree when you were thirteen, knowing the little, unused window to the attic never shut fully because it didn't lock right and because the walls of the house had moved. It was the way you could get in. That afternoon, it was the way you made your way in.

Your grandmother points to the small window.

Disapprovingly, Ophelia shakes her head. Her red hair as bright as a kiss.

The bark scratches your palms, and you hold tight enough for the pressure to inflict a modest hurt in your hands. Wind puts shivering into the large pecan. You have not climbed very high, but below, the fabric square stands out against the last vivid greens of the lawn. Your grandmother also appears smaller in her red blouse and her egg-blue skirt covered in Becky's coat, smaller and frailer, more away from you than you can ever remember her being. From this vantage, the world is minutia. Everything smaller than it could ever really, truly be. But not Ophelia. From so far up, against the whiteness, her red, red hair is the only thing you see.

Swiftly, your heart thumps, the little rhythm inside of it scattering and summoning courage, not revealing that you are nervous climbing this tree, afraid even, and wanting no one in the world to know. When you arrive at the branch your grandmother and you have identified as capable of wielding your weight, your body wraps its girth about the wood. Testing the strength of the branch is necessary. You test it. You wait. Steady yourself, you say. Don't move too fast. So you press this way and that and trust that what you know about steadiness is enough.

Once you've determined it's good, you give your grandmother a thumbs-up. As your arms gather the wood in their grasp, as you prepare to move farther away from the sureness of the trunk, a few pecans fall, and your grandmother moves quickly to step out of the way. Ophelia gathers a few of the nuts and places them in her bucket. Your grandmother flattens out the corners of the sheet.

When you shake more vigorously, then, then it rains.

Pecans pelt the white sheet. A meager showing at first. A sprinkling, soon a cascade. Then a deluge. You do this a few more times, and your grandmother and Ophelia catapult their voices and their laughter so that the tree doesn't seem so daunting.

After, Ophelia helps your grandmother gather the thin sheet's corners, the whole fabric bundles with nuts, and your grandmother watches you descend.

"Do you want the ladder?" she asks.

You decline.

Once the descent is manageable, you stare at the ground, and your heart pumps itself softly into the hole in your throat. You look around. The sky is a fury. The sky is orange like the flesh of autumn if autumn had a body and a beating heart and blood and air in its lungs. The sky is listening. The roof of the house glistens. The tree quivers, quakes. You feel a little bit cold again. And then, you jump.

"This is how we used to collect pecans," your grandmother says to Ophelia at the sink. "When I was a little girl."

In the kitchen, your grandmother rinses the pecans, and you ask where your uncle has gone. She ignores the question.

The water in the sink makes its metallic din.

Ophelia prepares sweet tea for your grandmother.

Destiny chases a pecan that wobbles across the floor. She'll busy herself with this for a while.

At first, your grandmother feigns not hearing. So you ask again. "Where is Tío? Do you know where he's gone?"

But she shrugs her shoulders and hums, focusing on cleaning the hard brown shells. The water splashes as it hits her hands in so many directions it juts and courses into the drain. She shrugs her shoulders and hums and rinses the pecans and asks you to check the dryer, because she does not want the clothes in it to wrinkle.

"The hangers. In the long closet. In the hallway."

Ophelia plays with Destiny, throws a green teddy bear and waits for the chubby dog to retrieve it, which she does, again and again, over and over. The bear flies, and the dog jumps. The bear squeals and is covered in matted drool.

Near Saint Michael, you think of the hangers, reaching for the knob of the closet door.

On most days, your grandmother's silence is brittle, can be broken, but now it's grown thicker. It's a silence much like the trunk of a tree, dense, impassable to most things.

The truth is, something has happened between you. You can't say what it is. You can't name it or grab it with your hands.

You grab the hangers and fold the T-shirts and socks and your uncle's underwear on the sofa.

Ophelia helps you.

21

On the day your mother left, you were three. It was the afternoon, and you were sleeping. You can't recall much, but you know that one day, after a tumult, after exchanging harsh, bitter words with your grandmother, your mother stuffed armfuls of her things into a backpack and a few white kitchen trash bags, which bloated like megamarshmallows as they filled with the quickly gathered belongings your mother would take when she left. You remember this was a time of great sadness, because your father had just died.

You remember the bags were fat like alabaster Jabba the Hutts, that they grew like plump little ghosts that could not stop themselves from consuming the happiness of the world. You were very young. You wondered if you, too, would fit in those bags. Where would your things go? How could she not want to take you, too?

You were old enough to know that something had gone terribly, terribly wrong.

You were not old enough to know the reasons adults do the things they do.

You were not old enough to know she was leaving you behind.

But why you fell asleep you will never be able to say.

It is a sleep you remember, though you were so young.

Sometimes you don't want to fall asleep at all.

Sometimes you wish you could stay awake forever. But you know that's unreal. You know that's unlikely and silly. You recognize sleep is good for you, vital for growth and bones and good, strong skin and clear thoughts, like the health teacher at school made you learn. You scored a 105 on that quiz—the new, improved you. *Good Job*, he scribbled at the top of your paper in green curled ink, near the score and beside your name.

God knows you are trying to do good.

That next morning when you awoke, the moon was still out, and your mother was gone. Like a pilot on a singular mission, you whizzed about the empty sky of the house, searching for her. A frantic trek. A trajectory that bounced the heart off the walls, over the sofas and tables, toward the roof and into the hard linoleum floors. You looked and looked. You sat by the door. You looked out the windows. But you never saw her again.

"Don't cry, *chiquito*," your grandmother whispered.

She held you as you cried. You cried hard that morning. Gray clouds cluttered the sky of your little huddled heart and outside, in the rest of the world, too. You didn't eat, and she had to go to work then, your grandmother, after a few days of watching over your despair. *Pokémon* played on TV. You were three or three and a half. A cousin, Leticia, came to watch you, and though she tried to get you to play games or watch movies or eat sweets, to do anything that might cause you to abandon your sadness, even if only temporarily, even if only for a minute, you sat plaintively in a wooden chair by the window, your mouth cemented by sobs, holding the red curtain of heaviness in your little fist all afternoon.

"She'll be back," Leticia claimed, rubbing her slim hands through your hair.

But you knew she was just saying this. Sometimes, no matter who you are or how old you've grown, you just know.

This is what you think of as you lay in bed on the night before your fight.

22

When you die, it is nothing like what they say it is like in movies and TV shows and books.

In fact, it happens much like an eyelid happens to your iris whenever you blink. Why are you blinking? It doesn't matter, because it just is. Like the last moment you are awake, before the sky becomes dark. In this way, the mind soothes the body into slumber, or the body does so to its thoughts, quells them, dims them into the one moment you are vivid and conscious and able to name things and then, then, you are not.

For you, it happened on a Thursday.

For you, it was supposed to be the chance to make something vast and enormous happen.

For you, it began with the little animal inside your heart, the livid one, the one made of rage and frustration and fear and wonder. What fears? That you were nobody and that there was nothing else in the world meant for you to do but be lonely, but lay in the noisy little bed that once belonged to your dad but not know and not see your reflection in your footsteps or in water. That little animal. It's the reason your uncle came back to live in your grandmother's house. It's the reason he took an interest in who you were and what you could do.

When you heard about the fight he could set up for you, you thought twice.

You really did.

You remembered what Becky had said all those times about earning things, waiting for them, paying your dues through hard work and patience, going without in order to come out good in the end. The other option? Going for broke. Running wild and leaping toward the first sign of fast money and breakneck success. For this reason, Becky decided you wouldn't work during high school, because if you gained the taste for money too early, it would spoil you, lure you away from schooling and a career and into a dependency that would be difficult later to step away from. "Money will do that," she said to your grandmother on the day you agreed you would wait until graduation to work.

When he finds you, you are sitting in your room with Destiny. She is chewing the little green bear Becky and your grandmother bought her on one of their trips to the Dollar Store. Destiny has gnawed off its ear, and the evidence, an amputated ear, sticks between her teeth.

"You gave me your word, Abraham," your Uncle Claudio reminds you that night, after the house has shut down and he has knocked on your door. He stands over you like a shelf with too much emptiness for you to decipher what it means or what it carries, what it offered you, really. You realize in that instant that no matter what you'd been taught, there was always that chance that the world really was better with whirlwind risk and big pay-offs, that trying and letting it all hang out might actually get you more than cowardice and caution, the playing it safe and taking it slow that Becky proposed. This is your uncle's way: quick and fast and brutal. In the middle of December, it is what he is serving you.

"Shouldn't you be at work?" you ask.

"I took the night off. For this. For your chance to start making it big. A fight. A chance," he explains, his two big hog hands pulled over his face like gloves, wiping at his eye slats, mopping his nose. "On the other side of Elmendorf. A little ranch with men who pay big to watch other men beat the shit out of each other. Only the strong survive. You're one of the strong, Abraham."

You ignore him. At first. It's what you told yourself to do. Though the idea of money before Christmas—what you might buy Ophelia, how you might alleviate some of your grandmother's stress over bills—smolders inside you.

"What you think? You game, Papo? I seen what you can do. You can be a beast."

Still, you try to ignore it. You say inside yourself, No. No. No.

"Eyes on the prize, Daddy. Look at me."

You avert your eyes.

But he pulls your chin toward his, makes you eye him.

Destiny stops toying with the little green bear, its stomach stitching ripped open, with white stuff jutting outward. She watches you.

"Eyes. On. The. Prize."

It's when you lock eyes, when you see yourself in those two dark puddles—that's when you know you are done.

∾ ∾ ∾

It happens faster than you'd like to admit. Your acceptance. The deal. But the drive to the ranch, the site of the fights, takes longer than you expect. Though once you've arrived, it doesn't take long to know you're in very deep.

There is a fire and accordion music rustling through a thicket. Mesquite and shrubs and thistle grow so heavy you cannot see through them. When he turns off the highway, your uncle checks his phone and drives you down a muddy road, chips of hardened soil flinging upward, striking the windshield and the doors. The sky is dark, each star peering down at the earth of which you are a part, this slick, crooked scene that you are soon to become part of.

"Today. Today is the beginning of everything we've been waiting for." Your uncle dips into himself for this notion, a consideration that pries itself from his lungs and maybe the liver, even, as internalized as perhaps an idea can become in order to convince you of its veracity. "Some people, Abraham, they're born with money. Born with opportunities. Born with every chance in the world to make it. But other people, they got to fight for everything they can get. And that's us. Life gives us a look, and you gotta take it, Papo. Because if you don't grab it, if you don't claim what's yours, somebody else will take your shit. And then you're left sitting on the sidelines, sucking your thumb, because someone else just took something that could have belonged to you."

It's a grip to your stomach. This way of seeing the world. The fear that he's right, and if you play your cards wrong, you're screwed for the rest of your life.

But nothing is easy, not for people like you. Your uncle says it, and Becky and your grandmother have acknowledged that, too. Some of us just have harder lives.

As the car approaches the ranch, the music amplifies. A man near a large fire is taking money. A small animal has been cooked, skewered with a long rod, and a man with a fat knife chisels chunks of meat from its flanks. A little goat, you think, as you drive nearer. Its tiny legs poking into the darkness, glowing. When your uncle exits the car, you think for a moment you might seize the keys, head off in the direction of the city and maneuver your way so far from this place. But instead, you wait for your uncle in his car. Your knuckles throb. Your heart quakes. You turn on the radio, spin the dial, nullify the sound inside you that thumps. You look up to the sky, at the salt of the stars, so many grains sprinkled across the blue-black night. You listen for country, and what you find is an old song, one you don't know.

But how can the moon be neon? you wonder. You look upward but the moon isn't even there.

By a tent, not too far from the little goat being carved, a couple of women drink and laugh vulgarly and show their parts to men, who pursue them into the unlit tent. You see the man taking your uncle's money point to the other side of the fire, and then he points to the tent and grabs your uncle's arms, and they both laugh. You hate that laugh. You note the light behind the fire is different, electric and suspended from seemingly endless wires attached to tall wooden posts. There is a house also and a stable for horses and a trailer attached to a dually truck. There is the stench of something burning, and you are afraid a few minutes later as your uncle approaches the car, adjusting himself, grinning big, staring back at the dark tent.

There was a time when you never would have trusted him. But that time was a hundred million miles away now, though you wish it was nearer, close enough to climb out of this car and run toward it, as fast as you can, no looking back, no regrets, no second thoughts.

If only . . .

For a couple hundred dollars, your uncle has bought your entry into a fistfight. In an hour, you'll vie for another three hundred if you can win.

"Who'm I fighting?"

"Doesn't matter. Some guy. And you're gonna beat his ass. No mercy, Abraham. And you're not gonna stop beating his ass until we have our money. That's what matters."

While he's building these words, you see yourself in the side mirror. It is possible: your lips ripped, your nose smashed, red fluid smothering your chin and purple neck, the whole front side of your torso as if it'd met head on with a tractor trailer, the gash in your forehead like a black hole in the deepest, darkest field of space. A dark sap oozing from this gash. In the mirror, you are not yourself, the old music dampening into the seat cloth, and you feel like generations of lost boys are staring back at you. You hope Ophelia will never see you this way.

And the fact is you never will see this guy. You'll never put your fists to his face or knock your knees into his mouth or make him lose teeth. Over time, you've wondered if this first guy existed at all, if it wasn't some ploy to get you in, so that you'd commit, so that you'd be game for what came next.

"Eleven thirty," your uncle says authoritatively. "That's what time you go in."

So you wait. You sit in the car and ogle your phone. Think of texting Ophelia, but then she'd ask where you were or what you were doing, and then you'd have to lie. You don't want to lie. You've mulled this over already. How you never want to lie to her. Contemplated it, jotted down the promise to yourself in your journal as you thought about your fight and the money and how everything would be different after this night while you waited for your uncle to shower and grab his shit, before you drove out to this godforsaken ranch. So you type the message, and the screen lights up the inside of the car. But the signal is weak, and it doesn't send.

In the car, you stare at the stars and listen to the sound of an accordion.

"You wanna watch the first fight?" your uncle taps on the window and asks.

Two guys are going at it underneath the electric lamps on the other side of the horses. You can hear a few cheers, but they do not last long, and then there are jeers and boos, and this, you conclude, is how these things end. A woman stumbles up behind your uncle and peers down at you.

"Who's this? What's your name?" she mumbles. Her lips are candy red.

But your mouth doesn't move, and your heart beats very fast. The line in your throat is pumping itself full and pronounced.

She almost falls over, but your uncle catches her.

She is drunk and unruly, and parts of her hair fall into her mouth.

"Be ready," he barks to you, and they laugh and head off into the tents with his hands all over her skin.

∾ ∾ ∾

Eventually, your time comes.

Everyone's time comes, you have learned.

But there's a hindrance, or a possibility, depending on how you view life.

"What if I told you there's a bigger payday?" your uncle, gripping the side of the door, leans in to mutter. "A real shot at something big. Bigger than we can imagine, Papo."

There isn't much time to decide. New opportunities are like this. Often you've only got seconds to make up your mind. And choices orchestrate life: we live and die by the choices we make, those we do not make.

"There's a bigger fight, Abraham, 2K. The guy on after you backed out, and now there's a slot. I have to tell you that's two thousand bones, Abraham. Imagine. Imagine what we could do."

You hear him out.

You hear the case that he makes.

You hear the line pounding in your neck, and you hear yourself say, No. No. No.

But he insists. But he opens the door and he holds your hand, and his voice is on you like a swarm of ants. You can hear the tears well up in his voice. He pleads. On his knees, he grabs your face, and your eyes go to him, and he lays it all out: "This is our chance."

Mud appears on your uncle's boots. You can see the puddles behind him glint, light from the ranch bouncing back into the sky, toward the clouds and the moon and the stars.

But this wasn't part of the deal. You know better than to go for more than you should.

"Anything you want. I can give you anything you want," he implores. His face swells and his eyes squint and his voice cracks. "I can tell you about your father."

"My father?"

"Yes. You have to go three minutes with this guy. Three minutes. You can dance circles 'round this pussy. Seems like a long time, but it ain't nothing, Papo. A hundred and eighty seconds. Three minutes. You got this. I know you got this. You just gotta stay moving for three minutes. Do you understand? Do you understand me, Abraham? Three minutes. Do that, and we get paid. Win this. I believe in you, Abraham. Do it for your dad."

Your uncle holds up three fingers. The fingers jut into the sky like crosses or light poles.

It's the beginning, and it is the end.

23

He was a bigger guy. Simple arithmetic. The mathematics of brawn. A man versus an almost-not-yet man. Built like a truck and without mercies. The last thing you remember: your teeth tasting dirt, the iron taste of wooziness and imbalance, and your uncle pushing you forward after two tremendous blows—your jaw like it had grown horrid wings and flown off your face—bringing you up to your knees, your uncle's fast fists telling you, "Go! Go! Go!" And so you see stars. You do. Just like you told Ophelia. Only the stars are nothing at all like the ones that cling to the Montezuma cypresses hanging down over the River Walk or the extrasolar ones, far away in the sky, those stars sending parts of themselves from across the universe, looking down on you with pity and love and apologies, calling you, whispering your name, lulling you with their little lilts of light, and as you shut your eyes, you remember this is your name. Your name. But at this point, at this hour, you won't know for certain if the stars are pulling you up or falling down into you, becoming you, or you becoming one of them. The rest, as they say, is silence.

24

It is amazing. That's what I can tell you about death. This silence. The most beautiful noise in the history of anyone's life. The brightest noise. For me, it is one moment, one that I'd forgotten, because that's what happens once all your days amass like a heap of hours and then a mountain of them, forming years and decades, maybe more. All the while, the brain is an organ as marvelous as the heart. We live and we forget and we learn and we see, and sometimes, we remember.

I died on a Thursday night in the middle of December.

I was seventeen.

I fell in love with a girl named Ophelia with the most marvelous red hair, a laugh like a sky full of birds, and a mother who'd lose her life in Afghanistan. On a ranch outside of San Antonio, I was beaten in a fight for two thousand dollars, because I couldn't move faster and couldn't strike any blows of my own and my eyes shut faster than my knuckles could strike out.

When my uncle drove me to the hospital, I still had a handful of minutes in my heart. Those minutes with their little patter and their rosebush of hopes. He balled up my shirt and used it to soak up the blood that made lines like a sloppy grid across the parts of my face that once kept my eyes and my nose and my mouth in their places. I heard him talking as he drove, and I listened as he sobbed a litany of apologies to me and to my father and to my mother, to my grandmother, to his own children, whom he'd abandoned somewhere along the way, to this car ride, in which I was not surviving the pummeling he'd arranged. Like this, I learned that my father had died because my Uncle Claudio sold him out to a heroin dealer to whom my crooked uncle owed a hive of money. My uncle told me this because he knew I was dying, because sometimes in life these are the only times the truth happens, when it's life and death and we can go either way. Perhaps this was his way of liberating himself of the heavy guilt he'd carried all of his life. He admitted that he'd led my father to an abandoned house by the southmost part of the river and watched my father get shot in the head. Perhaps my uncle needed to hear himself confess. Perhaps he absolved himself of all duty to truth and asked only for forgiveness in the seconds he believed he'd wronged me like he'd wronged my father like he'd wronged their mother so many times. Perhaps these were simply a muddle of lies, a feeble attempt meant to keep me holding on. Who knows?

What I know is he left me at the emergency room of Santa Rosa Hospital, stuttering to the nurse on duty that this was all gang shit and that I was his brother's one son, a lost boy who was breaking everyone's hearts, that I'd made it home barely, collapsing on his porch after some guys had jumped me—that he hoped they could save me, please, please. He offered my name and my grandmother's name, along with a too-vague description of these imaginary boys, and he left.

The doctors tried, and the nurses said my liver had lost its place in my body, that my lung had collapsed, that it had been punctured because my ribs were fractured and two of the ribs had punched through the wall of the lung. There was also damage to my spine and brain. They suspected I would die, and I did.

As I lay in the little room made of curtains, full of people who were realizing I was over, my grandmother laced her hand into my hand and called Ophelia, and Becky held my grandmother's hand, and my grandmother cried harder than all of the seas in all of the storms God ever made. Becky held her, and they prayed for me.

Sometimes I can still hear the curtains swaying, sometimes I can still hear Becky and my grandmother praying. It's a nice sound. Music, almost.

Did they know who'd done this? an officer asked my family.

No, said my grandmother.

No, repeated Becky. Not for sure, but maybe Claudio knew something, she told him as my grandmother fell into her palms, full of sobs and a sadness too many people in the world already know.

Ophelia sat with my grandmother and fanned her with a magazine.

But maybe is never a good enough answer.

But if something was going on, then Abram would have written it down in his journal, Ophelia thought as she climbed the pecan tree behind my grandmother's house and the wind beat on her face, her red, red hair clinging to her cheeks like a starfish asking the body to give it some life. Furtively she climbed, and the tree scraped the house, making itself heard. Inside, my uncle, immersed in hating himself, heard her climbing, and he decided it was nothing, as Ophelia survived the great tree and entered the house through the imperfect window of the attic.

He would have killed her, I now think, had he found her.

But she tiptoed through the house as he sat on the sofa with a gun to his head and the television screaming an old show about cowboys overtaking the West. Cowboys and Indians. Over the havoc inside himself, my uncle could not hear Ophelia gathering my backpack and collecting the pup, and before he could decide whether to commit to the trigger, Ophelia was gone.

It is amazing. That's what I can tell you about death. This silence. The most beautiful noise in the history of living. As bright as the lives of stars. For me, it is one moment, one that I'd forgotten, and in this moment, I am two, maybe three, and my father is driving, and I am sitting in my mother's lap in the front seat of his black Monte Carlo. He loved that car. It is New Year's, and my mother is smiling with every one of her white teeth as she counts down to midnight. She starts at ten and then nine . . . and my family is a family, and I sit in my mom's lap as my father drives us around the loop of four tight freeways that etch the perimeter of downtown in my city. There is no place like San Antonio. As the new year approaches, my father rolls down the windows, and the cold wind is in my face, too, opening every part of my eyes, and my mother is laughing her sweet laughter, counting down to four and to three. And it happens, slowly at first, and ardently, a few new stars popping up here and there, shrieking reds and chili-pepper yellows, blues as meaningful as the wholeness of the moon, striking emeralds running the sky's gamut in streaks, and soon, soon, the entire world around us is saturated with stars, because every neighborhood around me—the east, the west, the north, the south—is sending its fireworks high into the sky, the children shooting their laughter and their awe to soar above skyscrapers and freeways and above the Tower, and there are so many people in their yards and in the streets, loving, enjoying, seeing the magic of the sky, and this way, in my mother's lap, with my father reaching over to kiss her before she can say one, with their arms around me, my father says, "Happy New Year, baby. I love you," and he kisses us both, my mother and my father breathing happiness as if it were air, and the world is perfect, and the world is mine, the moon is watching, and the world is made of light.

ACKNOWLEDGMENTS

Thank you to the Macondo Writers' Workshop for offering
support, opportunity and inspiration. In addition, thank you,
Reyna Grande, Natalia Treviño, Richard Villegas, Jr., Rafa
Esparza and Vicki Grise, for feedback and guidance.